C0060 42816

Born in São Paulo, Patricia Melo has published
eight novels including *The Killer*, which won
the Deux Ocenas prize, and *Inferno*, winner
of the Iabuti Prize. More recently *Black Waltz*

libraries

Pollokshaws Library
50/60 Shawbridge Street
Glasgow G43 1RW
Phone: 0141 276 1535

This book is due for return on or before the last date shown below. It may be
renewed by telephone, personal application, fax or post, quoting this date,
author, title and the book number.

WORLD CRIME DISPLAY 2019

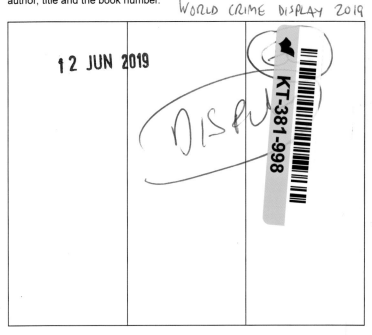

1 2 JUN 2019

DISPL

KT-381-998

Glasgow Life and its service brands, including Glasgow
Libraries, (found at www.glasgowlife.org.uk) are operating
names for Culture and Sport Glasgow.

Glasgow
CITY COUNCIL

THE BODY SNATCHER

Patrícia Melo

Translated by Clifford E. Landers

BITTER LEMON PRESS
LONDON

BITTER LEMON PRESS
First published in the United Kingdom in 2015 by
Bitter Lemon Press, 47 Wilmington Square, London WC1X 2ET

www.bitterlemonpress.com

First published in Portuguese as *Ladrão de cadáveres*
by Editora Rocco Ltda, Rio de Janeiro, 2010

© Patrícia Melo 2010
English translation © Clifford E. Landers 2015

Published by arrangement with Literarische Agentur Dr. Ray-
Güde Mertin Inh. Nicole Witt e. K., Frankfurt am Main, Germany

All rights reserved. No part of this publication
may be reproduced in any form or by any means
without written permission of the publisher

The moral rights of the author and the translator
have been asserted in accordance with the
Copyright, Designs and Patents Act 1988

All the characters and events described in this
novel are imaginary and any similarity with real
people or events is purely coincidental.

A CIP record for this book is available from the British Library
ISBN 978–1–908524–539
eBook ISBN 978–1–908524–546

Typeset by Tetragon, London
Printed and bound by CPI Group (UK) Ltd, Croydon, CR0 4YY

Bitter Lemon Press gratefully acknowledges the
financial assistance of the Arts Council of England

This work is published with the support of the Ministry
of Culture of Brazil/ Fundação Biblioteca Nacional.
Obra publicada com o apoio do Ministério da Cultura
do Brasil / Fundação Biblioteca Nacional.

Supported using public funding by
ARTS COUNCIL
ENGLAND
LOTTERY FUNDED

MINISTÉRIO DA CULTURA
Fundação BIBLIOTECA NACIONAL

For Pedro Henrique

Cadavers cannot bear to be nomads.

TOMÁS ELOY MARTÍNEZ

Part I

THE CADAVER

1

We flounder in the heat.

I hear steps nearby on the neighboring terrace but don't have the energy to shout.

They whisper, trip, and break something. Laugh.

Downstairs, the bicycle shop is closed. The kids, in bands, amuse themselves by spying on the neighbors in the area. They hang from trees, climb on roofs, squeeze through gaps. In the distance I hear the sound of shopping carts ripping up the asphalt. They screech.

Those goddamn bogus Indians, says Sulamita, getting up nude and going into the bathroom.

Down below, the old woman yells. The Indian woman. Just yesterday she told me she knows how to braid acuri palm straw.

Sulamita gets irritated when she sleeps with me. She says I have to look for a job, get away from here, find another area to live. That shitty bunch of Indians, she says.

I like the place. And I like Corumbá. And I've gotten used to the children, who often take advantage of my absence to go through my things. I also like the old Indian woman and think of her when I go fishing.

I hear Sulamita filling a bucket of water in the bathroom. Don't do it, I say, to no avail. On tiptoe, she approaches the door and catches the children by surprise with their backs turned, perched on the window ledge.

I hear the kids running, shouting and laughing, after the soaking they got.

Only then do I open my eyes.

It's Sunday.

2

The reporter says: thirty-three thousand young people will be murdered in the next four years. In my mind I see a policeman opening fire on them. The blacks. Shot from behind, in my imagination. The poor. I see brain matter clinging to the wall where the massacre takes place. And the edges of the wounds. The reporter says: the dead, according to statistics, will be black and brown. Someone will have to hose down the sidewalks, I think.

I like to get in my clunky red van, turn on the radio, and in the comfort of the same-old, same-old, after a cold shower and some strong coffee, listen to the announcer talk about the drop in the stock market somewhere in the world, massacres, earthquakes, Taliban attacks, kidnappings, floods, homicides, pandemics, rapes, and mile-long traffic jams. It calms me down. It's part of my recovery to think like that. I hear all of it with the good sensation that I'm not the target of anything, I'm outside the statistics, I'm not rich, I'm not black, or Muslim, that's what I think, I'm safe, protected in my van as I proceed toward the town of Remédios and turn onto the Old Highway, always with the windows open for the smell of the woods to invade my nostrils.

Sometimes Sulamita sleeps at home, and on those days I run my private antivirus listening to the stories about what goes on at the police precinct where she's an administrative assistant. Drug busts, arrest warrants, raids, corruption, and fraud. People fuck themselves up royally, that's the truth. Today, while we were eating freshly baked bread, she told me about the woman who showed up at the precinct with a knife sticking out of her ear.

That's how I began that Sunday. So far no problems, I told myself. At least I don't have a knife in my ear. We're doing well. Control, over.

I parked on the first bridge, got out and went down to the mouth of the canal and stayed there, listening to the croaking of the frogs and thinking about where I would go fishing.

I remembered the day Sulamita and I rode our bicycles to the grotto. A stupid idea, Sulamita said. The road was swamped from the rains, the mud was up to our ankles. Sulamita complained as she pushed her bike during the trip. Later, we bathed in the icy waters of the grotto.

From the bridge almost no animals were visible, not even cavies or alligators, because of the ranches in the vicinity. A few toucans and magpies were flying over the low vegetation in search of food in the pools of water reflecting the sunlight.

It was so hot that the trucks transporting cattle in the region weren't risking it. Sweat was pouring down my face.

I went back to the van and plunged into the woods, among the caranda palms. I continued as far as the trail permitted, taking the whole fishing caboodle – reel, pole, and hooks – along with a cooler full of beer, and some peanut candy.

After leaving the van parked under a tree, I walked to the Paraguay River, carrying my fishing materials and the net. I don't know how far I walked. My head was throbbing under the sun. On the way, I stopped at the mouth of the grotto, the same one I visited with Sulamita. Exhausted, I took off my clothes and for a long time floated, savoring the coolness on my body, until my forehead stopped throbbing.

Feeling better, I followed the trail to the river.

It was January, when the fish come up in schools to lay their eggs in the headwaters of the river. During that time, fishing is prohibited: you can't use cast nets, seines, or stake nets. The advantage was that I had the place all to myself.

I sat down, opened a beer. It was one of those calm, bright Sundays when your thoughts wander without destination or worry.

I spent the afternoon like that, a little groggy from the beer, watching the river flow. A warm breeze blew over my body.

I caught all the fish it was possible to carry on the trek back to the van. Less than ten kilos: two pacu, a *surubí*, and three *piavuçu*s.

Later I stretched out in the shade, ate a bit of the candy, and dozed off, waiting for the temperature to drop for the walk back. I don't know how long I slept. I dreamed that I had to survey phone lines and coordinate the operators through the radio hookup, over, which was making a horrible squeal. All of that had been a long time ago, and yet the radio was still in my nightmares.

I woke up with my heart racing, hearing the sound of an engine. I looked toward the sky and saw the airplane flying low, thinking it was doing aerial photography.

I don't really know how it all happened. Suddenly, an explosion, and the plane plunged like a kingfisher into the Paraguay.

3

The nose of the single-engine plane was underwater in the narrowest and most irregular part of the Paraguay, an unnavigable shallow stretch where one of the wings had buried itself. Dark smoke was coming from the engine.

I removed my pants and sneakers and swam to the aircraft. The water level was a little above my waist. As soon as I climbed onto the fuselage I spotted the pilot, a large guy, young, with a bony face. Blood was gushing from the wound to his forehead.

I forced open the right-hand door, partially out of the water, and went inside. I told the pilot not to worry, I'd take him to my van and we'd find help using my cell phone. You're very lucky, I said while I undid his safety belt, very, very lucky, dropping out of the sky and still being alive.

That was the moment when he bought it, just as I was saying he was a fortunate guy. First he emitted a muffled sigh, almost a moan. I checked his pulse. Nothing.

A feeling of terror swept over me.

Water was starting to rise into the plane. I opened the right-hand door to keep us from being dragged away, uncertain if my reasoning was correct.

Panting, swallowing water, I swam back to the riverbank, now fearing the piranhas. I tried to turn on the cell phone in my pants pocket, but couldn't get a signal.

I returned to the plane, went into the cabin and sat down

in the copilot's seat. I stayed there for some minutes hearing the water beat against the fuselage, pondering what to do. Maybe the best thing would be to take the youth away from the river. Still, there wasn't the slightest chance that I could carry him to the van. He was heavier than me and probably weighed eighty kilos. I could have dragged him, but the idea of dragging a corpse bothered me.

It also occurred to me that it would make no difference if I left him there for the rescue team.

From the road I could call the police. They'd arrive in less than three hours.

I checked the young man's pulse. That was when I noticed the leather backpack hanging by a strap behind the seat.

Inside I found an unmistakable package, one of those you see on television in stories about drug busts. A compact mass, white and crumbly, wrapped in heavy plastic and sealed with adhesive tape. I made a small hole in the wrapping and tested the powder by rubbing it on my gums. I was no expert in the subject, but I wasn't a novice either. Even my tongue went numb. My throat too.

I sat there, thinking about the police station I'd have to pass on the way to Corumbá. The thought of a pile of money made me take less than a minute to decide.

I don't know who said that a man by himself isn't honest for long, but it's the gospel truth.

Driven by the same impulse, I also took the pilot's wristwatch, and got the hell out of there.

4

A year earlier I was telemarketing manager in a boiler room in São Paulo, responsible for the sale of exercise equipment, the kind that you fold up, put under the bed, and never use again. I had sold worse things, like credit cards, water filters, and weight-loss girdles. I was living at my limit, bloated with coffee, running back and forth in the aisles like a frightened rabbit, preparing reports and coordinating sales teams by radio, always with the feeling that I wouldn't be able to deliver the goods.

Part of my job description was to teach new operators to use PowerPoint, Word, Excel, and Outlook, a long and demanding training process that invariably served to trigger my migraine attacks. I had just finished instructing a very young and inexperienced employee, and on her very first day at the phone desk, in the morning, when I went to monitor her initial calls, I saw that she was having trouble pronouncing the words. And this after going through the ordeal of training. What's that in your mouth? I asked.

And then she showed me the piercing she'd put in the tip of her tongue the day before.

What killed me was her expression. She smiled, ill at ease, as if she'd done something naughty. Or as if it was possible to work like that, lisping, spitting the words at people who don't want to talk to us, who hang up in our faces when they realize it's about sales. You're selling something? So long, they say. I'm not interested. I don't want to buy anything. And they slam the phone down in our faces. And her, my employee, with a stud in her tongue.

How are you going to communicate with our customers? I asked.

She smiled, embarrassed, tossing her head back.

All I remember is a wave of hatred rising in my body and the slap I gave her.

Everyone believed I was a tense kind of guy but under control. I thought so myself.

The first thing that occurred to me at that moment was that we never understand how a responsible, hard-working citizen pulls a gun and kills a driver in a traffic argument. Actually, it's very simple. It happens in the same way that I struck my employee. The gun is there, in the glove box. Suddenly some young guy cuts you off at an intersection, you jump out of the car and put a bullet in his forehead. It's that simple.

I immediately took the girl to my office. She was frightened, me even more so. Drink some water, I said, sit here, use this handkerchief. I apologized in every way possible. But I wasn't able to forgive myself, much less understand how I'd been capable of acting like that with the girl. She remained quiet, her eyes on the floor. Like a dog that's been swatted. She had just the one torn suit, which she had shown up wearing ever since the first day of training. A clean and threadbare girl. Pale. She looked like a bottle of water. Empty. You've seen plenty of her type around, very common. With a cheap purse, waiting at the bus stop, pushing buttons in elevators, selling tickets at the movies. That day, she was trying not to burst into convulsive sobs in front of me. Can I go to the bathroom? she asked. The two of us there, facing each other, and I didn't know what to do. Forgive me, I said. A thousand pardons. I offered my bathroom, managers have that privilege, but she preferred to use the employees'. She returned five minutes later, without the piercing, no makeup, and asked permission to go back to her desk.

The next few days were terrible. It was as if the two of us had committed some crime. The atmosphere between us was so heavy that she could barely manage to say good morning to me. I even avoided going by her desk out of remorse and embarrassment. I waited for her to denounce me. In bed at night, I couldn't sleep, thinking about the possibility. But she didn't inform on me.

That lasted a week. On the eighth day, the girl didn't show up. Seeing her chair empty, I had a bad premonition. Soon afterward, someone from her family called and we learned she had thrown herself from the tenth floor.

At the funeral, from a distance I saw her husband with spiked hair and an exotic appearance, with rings in his ear and nose, their two-year-old daughter in his arms.

It wasn't because of me, I know. She already had her eye on the abyss. I merely provided the impulse for her to jump.

Just who was that girl? my boss asked when he returned from a trip and heard the news. Days later, the story of the slap was known by all the salespeople, who refused to listen to my orders or talk to me. The news spread like a virus throughout the building and beyond. Workers on other floors, for other firms, turned away in the elevator or in the cafeteria where I had lunch every day. And they whispered when I passed by. It was because of him, they said. The slap. I became a kind of celebrity. The guy who slapped. I was the plague, the devil. Someone wrote on the bulletin board: "Out, heartless monster!"

I have no choice, the general manager said when he fired me.

I quickly went into a tailspin. I couldn't get out of bed and was taking so many sleeping pills that I was like a machine that they turned on and off.

You look awful, my cousin Carlão said when, by chance, he visited me in São Paulo. And by chance he invited me to spend some time with him.

That was how I moved to Corumbá. By chance.

5

One point one kilos, according to the bathroom scale. They say in the States it would be worth twice as much, three times as much in Europe, but I had no plans to take it further. Or the courage. Actually, I didn't give a shit about money. I just wanted enough to not have to work for some time longer.

I weighed the drugs twice more to make sure of the amount.

I returned everything to the backpack, climbed on a chair, opened the cover that allows access to the crawl space, and placed the pack behind the water tank.

My room is on the outskirts of Corumbá and belongs to the son of the chief of the Guató tribe, who neither speaks Guató nor knows how to canoe.

The space is larger than my previous address, a hovel looking out on Highway 26A, where there was nothing but toads and scrub. It was hard for me to get used to that place, with flies buzzing around, mud, and backlands people with nothing to offer except brotherhood. I felt empty there, at night with my eyes closed, I couldn't forget the noise in São Paulo or my office on Avenida São Luiz with its peeling walls lit by the neon sign of the fitness center across from my window.

I sometimes still dream about my salesgirl who committed suicide, her pale face, and wake up at the sound of the slap, as if someone were attacking me. But now I think of

São Paulo as a kind of atomizer that transformed me into something tiny, weak, and breakable, capable of slapping my employee in the face. A true sickness, that city. Like those that attack soldiers when they put on a uniform and head off to war. Or subordinates, when they follow orders. Not that you like being on the battlefield or obeying orders. It's more a question of consistency; after all, you're there to accomplish certain things. You've got to adjust. And fast, we fit in. It could have been worse, I think. I could have killed a driver in traffic. Cooked the books. Stolen money. Or thrown myself from the tenth floor. In any case, I had fallen into the well, sunk, and rotted like a tomato dropped on the ground at an outdoor market. I had barely gotten away. It was in those terms that I thought about that city. I promised myself never to return to that life. Never again, over.

It was Rita, my cousin's wife, who helped me out of the hole. The first time I saw her, she was sunbathing in a bikini, near the gasoline pump, and already at that moment I could sense sparks of electricity coming from her body to burn mine. She was twenty-six and sold cosmetics door to door. She wasn't pretty. But there was something about her face that pleased everybody at first sight. When Carlão spoke to me about her the first time, saying that for her he had left his wife and daughters, he spoke precisely of that aspect of Rita, her curiosity, her smile, her laughter, and he described her very well. Her nose was a bit large; her hair was dyed; her feet small and bony; but you didn't pay attention to any of that when you were beside her.

When Carlão went shopping or traveled, she would come down to the pump and keep me company. She would come up to my room with fresh coffee. We would go swimming in a nearby lake. This place is the end of the world, she said. Last stop. Just look where you ended up. Take one more step, you'll drop into the beyond. If you go in the wrong direction, you'll wind up in Bolivia.

We sometimes remained quiet, side by side, smoking and gazing at the empty highway, until one day she asked me who the girl was who called me every day. Our faces were so close together that I could almost smell the coffee on her breath. My girlfriend, I said. And Sulamita is the name of a person? she asked. I thought it was some kind of mineral found in the region. Aluminum phosphate, those things. I laughed. She remained serious and said she was falling in love with me.

I moved out the next day. I didn't want any problems with my cousin.

Now there I was, unemployed and with a kilo of cocaine hidden in the crawl space.

Before taking a shower, I went downstairs, crossed through the hallway beside the bicycle shop, and offered the fish to the old Indian woman, the bike shop owner's mother. Serafina was her name.

There were other Guatós in the neighborhood. I saw them there, with their slanted eyes, their flip-flops, playing football in the late afternoon, doing labor of every kind, bodywork on cars, security, cleaning. They were no longer accustomed to life on the island from which they had been expelled by the army and to which they were later able to return when priests in the region began raising a fuss to defend them. Serafina preferred the city after her husband was hospitalized with heart problems.

The only problem was living with her son, she said, now that the old chieftain had died. The family lived crowded into two rooms. Serafina slept in the kitchen with her three grandchildren, jammed against the couple's bedroom. There were small mattresses leaning against the walls and clothes drying behind the refrigerator. Grease from the bicycle shop was gradually making its way into the house and up the walls.

The daughter-in-law wasn't part of the tribe and got irritated when the old woman spoke Guató. Their mother would slap the little Indians for any reason, and now and then would hit Serafina, who would be expelled onto the sidewalk as punishment.

On those occasions I took her to my room. She would be confused, disoriented. Do you think, she asked, it was because I went into the refrigerator? I got a banana. Was it because of the banana?

They all went to the supermarket, she said that night. They'll be back soon, with cans and crackers, she added, sighing. I have some fried sausage here. Do you want it?

I thought it would be better not to leave the house, with all that powder going tick-tock in my head like a time bomb.

I ate in a hurry, thanked her, and went back to my room to see if there was anything on television about a missing plane.

6

The news I was waiting for didn't appear till mid-morning. The reporter affirmed that the pilot had been missing since Sunday. His name was José Beraba Junior, which I knew from the documents I'd found in his backpack. What I didn't know was that the young man was the son of a wealthy cattle rancher in the region. The images showed the pilot in an equestrian competition, skiing in Aspen, and vaccinating cattle with his father. They said the search for the disappeared single-engine plane would focus on the area in the vicinity of Corumbá where, according to radar, the last contact had been made at around four o'clock on Sunday afternoon. Concluding the coverage, a statement from his girlfriend. I know Junior is alive, she said, and I ask everyone to pray for him.

So far so good, I thought. Everything under control, over.

I dragged up a chair, reached the crawl space, and took out the pilot's backpack.

Calmly, I spread the contents on the table and once again carefully noted each of the objects: watch, glasses, wallet, keys, cell phone, two pens. And the package of drugs.

In the wallet I found several credit cards, two hundreds and three tens in cash, and the pilot's personal documents. There was also a membership card from the Cattle Raisers Association of Mato Grosso do Sul.

It would be wise for me to get rid of everything, toss the pack in the river after weighting it down with stones.

I decided I would do that the next time I went fishing.

I put the watch on my wrist and stored the other objects in the backpack before returning it to the crawl space.

As I was getting dressed, I remembered a pawnshop that belonged to an old Arab, near the Santa Cruz cemetery, where I had hocked my mother's wedding ring when I first came to Corumbá.

At eleven, the city shuttered under the sun. I parked behind the cemetery, and as soon as I got out of the car my glasses fogged up. I arrived at the pawnshop bathed in sweat, and offered the Arab the watch.

He carefully examined the green sticker with a hologram on the back of the watch, where the serial number was.

Then he ran some figures on his calculator and offered me an amount that I promptly accepted, happily signing the pawn ticket.

I went back to the car patting the money in my pocket, thinking that at least for the time being I could get by.

Before going home, I bought a precision scale, plastic bags, adhesive tape, and a sackful of red stars.

They would be my trademark, over.

Around seven o'clock, I parked in front of the police precinct and waited for Sulamita. She came out, accompanied by detective Joel. Ciao, Sweetheart, he said. Ciao, Tranqueira, a nickname that means albatross. That was how they addressed each other. Sweetheart and Tranqueira.

On the way home we bought a pizza. We ate with the television on, drinking beer, with me paying careful attention to the news.

Later, in bed, I tried to get some information out of Sulamita that was important to my new undertaking. I lined

25

up questions one after the other, calmly, so as not to draw attention to them. Along the way, I embedded some words of praise. And kisses, over. And then the questions started up again.

That was how I learned that the drug setup in Corumbá was no different from the rest of Brazil, which meant there were no more cartels or mafias, only a network of businessmen who mixed in a single bundle auto dealerships, cattle ranches, auto parts retailers, slaughterhouses, chop shops, warehouses, air taxis – all with the aim of facilitating the drug traffic. It was hard to break into that setup. You had to have things, and I had nothing. You had to know the right people, and I wasn't even from Corumbá. That's how it works in wholesale, Sulamita said, adding that in retail the traffickers didn't follow any specific pattern. That's my approach, I thought. Small-scale, over. There are people who work alone, said Sulamita, mules recruited here in the backlands, the unemployed, people in debt who agree to haul the drugs wherever. Those are the ones we catch in a bust. I mean, I'm not talking about myself. I don't do any of that. Administrative assistant is a position without any specific role. You plug holes doing what the others don't want to do or don't like doing. That's my routine. I'm always up to my neck in investigations and taking statements, dealing with what I call the "I dunno" crowd. The guy doesn't know anything. Never saw the victim. Never killed. Never robbed. Wasn't even in the city the day of the crime. Nothing to declare. I'm sick of all that, Sulamita said. I'm getting out; I've taken the exam for chief of autopsy.

It was almost eleven when my cell phone rang. It was Rita.

I feel sad, she said, I can't even eat. Can I come over there? I had the impression she was drunk.

Wrong number, I answered.

Are you with Sulawhatshername?

No one here by that name, I said.

I doubt that you don't think about me.

She hung up.

Sulamita was nearby and I was afraid she had overheard.

Wrong number, I said.

I don't know if she believed me. At least, she didn't say anything.

We slept together that night. Or rather, Sulamita slept. I stayed awake, staring at the ceiling and thinking. About the cadaver, over.

A horrible thing, falling out of the sky and dying like that.

7

The sun reigned over everything without pity. People ran as if it were possible to escape the heat. Here and there you could see asphalt melting. In that city, life was like that, the sky blue, the ground steaming, and people trying to flee the furnace. Here things rot faster, that's what they say. More worms, over.

I parked the car at the corner and observed the mansion that occupied the entire block, with its palms positioned geometrically, as if they were soldiers. I counted twelve soldiers. Toward the rear, the door to the barracks. They were there, I thought, gathered and desperate. Waiting for the fallen warrior.

A uniformed guard opened the iron gates, and a police car left the locale.

In the garden, two dogs who looked more like sheared goats sluggishly watched the youth cleaning the pool with a long pole. Flies buzzed.

What the hell was I doing there?

At night, tossing in bed, the idea that I was beside the pilot at the exact moment of his death and, worse still, that I had been capable of robbing the dead, came back to haunt me, frighten me, fill me with terrible foreboding. It was as if it had made us partners, over. Me and the cadaver. Suddenly, he was one of my problems. Him and all that cocaine in my crawl space. And that was when it struck me as an excellent idea to go to the family's house and leave an anonymous letter with a map showing the site of the crash. Follow the Old Highway, take the trail with the carnaubas. The path dotted in red with precise markings would guide the family. It took me almost an hour to draw the map. An X marking the spot. Your son died here. P.S. He didn't suffer, over.

More than the image of the cadaver abandoned in the river, what agonized me was thinking what was going on inside that house. We're sure he's all right, his girlfriend had said on television. The mother crying. That I understand, over. Mothers who deteriorate like that, rotting away from so much crying. Before learning that people die, I learned that they disappear. They move away from home and evaporate. They leave us perplexed, looking at the empty bed, which is almost like a scream, a clubbing in the morning. You dream about them every night. Dream they're alive, dream they call, dream they're coming home. Always the same dreams; you end up actually believing they're alive. And there's also the research, which says that seventy percent of the disappeared return. You may no longer believe in God, but you believe in research. You cling to those percentages as if they were a prayer. And the numbers, along with the dreams, make that person into a kind of living-dead. A zombie. I knew all of that very well.

Even today I couldn't think of my mother as someone who made wedding cakes, decorating with icing the steps that lead to the rococo top where the sugar bride and groom smile eternally. I remembered her as almost a bleeding attachment of the telephone that was constantly close by. Waiting for my father to call and say he hadn't died or abandoned us or lost his memory. That he was alive. That he was going to return. Almost twenty years later, more dead than alive, my mother still kept the phone in her lap and waited.

The truth is that the dead need to really die. They need to be put in the coffin and buried. Or incinerated. You have to be there when the last shovelful of dirt is tossed in.

What the hell was I doing there? The ideas that come forth in the night, all of them, the ones that seem good and the ones that seem bad, are always terrible. False alarms. Deceptive advertising. Consumer alert: don't try to do this while awake. A map of the site of the accident? What did I care if they were suffering? I didn't even know those people.

After the guard disappeared into the garden, with the dogs trailing him, I went to the gate and watched the guy cleaning the pool. He didn't appear to be in any hurry. The tragedy inside there had nothing to do with his dead leaves. Or with the chlorine being thrown into the pool. And there was still a lawn that went on forever to tend to, with pergolas and clusters of plants that weren't normally seen in Corumbá.

If I wanted to help, the best thing would be to call the police. Anonymously. Or the family itself. At least it was a way of settling accounts with the cadaver, who had given me all that cocaine as a gift. Although he hadn't really given me anything. As the saying goes, finding isn't stealing. The truth is, I didn't owe anyone. There was no reason for me to get involved with those people.

I lit a cigarette, thinking that maybe, one day, someone would come by my house to say where my father's body was. In an abandoned lot behind a cement factory. At the bottom of the river. With two bullets in his head. Buried in a backyard on the outskirts.

Are you the driver? asked the guard, appearing suddenly before I had a chance to escape.

I could say I was just looking at the garden. Beautiful lawn, isn't it? My roses are parched. The daisies died. Nothing thrives in this sun. It wouldn't have been at all difficult to start a conversation or get out of there, but out of fright I said yes and was led toward the mansion. On the way, I gathered my courage. That's why I'm here, I thought. I'm going in there to tell everything. The image I had of them was like a dog that has to be put down. I'm going to end their dark hope. Go inside and do it right, I told myself. Go there and deliver the coup de grâce, over.

Care for something to eat? Dalva, the cook, a short woman with thick legs, was eating roast beef and kale, her elbows supported on the table. She wiped her plate with pieces of bread. With her mouth full, she told me the story of the young man. He had gone to spend the weekend at the ranch of a friend. He called on Sunday after lunch advising that he would arrive in an hour. He liked to fly. He was always flying around the savanna. To buy drugs, I thought. From Bolivians.

Half an hour later, I was taken to an office with lots of pictures of the family. And of cows exhibited at fairs. Prizewinners. I sat there, alone. Father and son embracing, on the wall. The boots of the two are identical, attention-grabbing, I noted. Hereditary boots. The watch I pawned is on the boy's wrist.

Suddenly, the screaming began. It was a woman's voice. I don't care a bit what they're going to do, she said, you're the father and it's you, you, it's you who have to do something, I want my son back, bring my son back.

The door was shut, but it was still possible to hear the she-wolf howling. They're all alike, she-wolves. The same howls that cut deep down inside you like a razor.

Shortly afterward, the man in the photo came into the office, wearing the same boots as in the picture. He seemed confused. He said we had already spoken by telephone. Yesterday, he said.

31

I said that it must have been another driver. But he didn't hear me. He was in a hurry. I already have information about you, excellent information.

I was there to tell him about the accident. After all, that was why I had come into that house. To speak about the explosion and the crash. To kill the hopeless dog. I can take you to the scene, I thought of saying. It's shitty to feel sorry for others. I stood there, my finger on the trigger, and ended up accepting the job and agreeing on a good salary.

When can you start? he asked.

Tomorrow.

I left thinking that at any moment I could call and come up with some excuse. Or simply not show up. Disappear from the map.

And it's exactly because of this that we fuck up our lives. We always think we can get out in time.

8

Reeeck, the chain echoes. All that grease made Moacir even blacker. The noise was irritating me. Squatting on the sidewalk, the Indian was trying to fix the chain of the bicycle of the young man, drunk beside him, who was amusing himself with the neighborhood dogs. Listless squalid animals so ugly it pained you to look at them. The dogs and the men. Dirty tatters. They barked. They pissed against posts. Reeeck. The sun was murder.

As Moacir was moving the pedal, jerkily turning the chain, the bicycle's handlebars came loose. Damn, said the drunk, bursting out laughing. Better off tossing the whole thing in the trash, I thought.

I closed the window and lay down on the bed. I reread the note that Rita had left with Serafina that morning. Reeeck. Reeeck. "Thanks for hanging up in my face. Today is my birthday. You – just you, you alone – are invited to the party, at nine o'clock. Signed, Rita."

I opened a can of beer and – reeeck – thought about what to do.

It would be nice to cool off in the chilly waters of the grottoes, but I felt too heavy to float. Very hot. I thought several times about calling the pilot's family and backing out. The problem was that returning to São Paulo wasn't part of my plans. Not even for business. I had already wandered under the Corumbá sun with the classified ads in my hand, looking for something like Carlão's gas station, where he did everything from manning the pump to patching tires, with time to sit in the shade and let my thoughts wander, and all I had found was bakeries and backyard hydraulic pump shops. And other crap. Everything hot. Nothing for me. But the job in the rancher's home was good. At least I'd have air conditioning, and that counted for a lot in Corumbá. WE HAVE AIR CONDITIONING, businesses wrote on ornamental plaques to attract customers. Ten degrees cooler is the formula for happiness in those parts. That's what they were giving me: a good car, with air conditioning, to drive. Besides which, what did it matter that it was the house of the pilot that I had seen die? What did it matter that I had abandoned his body in the river? I didn't kill anyone, over. Even if I had pulled the youth from the plane and carried him on my back to the city, nothing would have changed. He'd be dead all the same. We're all going to die someday. What did it matter if I had swiped the coke? Let him throw the first stone, over. All of us steal something at some time or other. Almost all. At least once. Or we're going to steal. Brazil is full of pricks, that's for sure.

In the evening, calmer, I took a cold shower, removed the drugs from the crawl space, and got to work. I had decided I would sell the powder, make some money, and that would be that. A single sale. Without taking chances, because that's how people fuck themselves. What was temporary becomes a permanent way of doing things. You start making money and somebody feels cheated. Somebody you owe or who owes you. Or is simply envious. A nosy neighbor. An instant enemy. The ones who come out of nowhere without you even noticing. Some guy you treated badly. And he calls the police and blows the whistle on you. Sulamita had said the same thing: catching criminals has little to do with the competence of investigators. Rather, nothing to do. It's purely see-something-say-something, she said. 800-STOOLIE. People call us giving the name and address of the traffickers. The whole record. In the drug trade, she said, only one thing is absolutely guaranteed: someone is going to rat you out. You stand in line, waiting. It's like owning a motorcycle: one day for sure you'll have an accident. You might not die, but you're going to fall. That's the way it works. Therefore, I thought, no getting fired up over easy money. No buying more blow. That package was a present, nothing more. A gift from the cadaver. That was the most complicated part, thinking that my luck, the good things that happened to me at that moment, the drugs and the job, had to do with the deceased. Chance? A sign? Whatever it was, it would be an unforgivable sin not to grab the opportunity. That's something I had learned in my life as a salesman.

The work of weighing and wrapping the powder helped me arrange my thoughts. I placed a gram in each envelope and sealed it with the red star. I'd seen that in a film, and it struck me as an effective strategy. My customers would right away associate the star with coke free of marble dust, glass, talc, or amphetamines. And I would also sell cheap. That's the logic of business – better and cheaper.

Once the Indian stopped making noise, I opened the window again. At the corner, the knife-sharpener arrived with his equipment attached to an old bicycle. Three housewives gathered around him, holding colored parasols. Sparks flew from the grindstone, along with a buzzing that pierced my head like needles. Or bees.

A little later, the children returned from school in bevies. Moacir closed the bicycle shop. Men on their way home stopped at the corner bar. The street quickly filled with urchins laughing and running around in packs, playing football.

I smoked a cigarette and watched the sun set behind the house. The temperature started to become bearable.

At seven forty-five, Moacir appeared on the sidewalk and asked if he could speak to me. I gestured for him to come up.

He had bathed, but the grease had impregnated his skin. His sweat was dark, oily. His hair, a shiny mass. Skinny legs, sunken shoulders. He didn't look like a chieftain's son, and he'd be screwed if he were forced to hunt a jaguar like his ancestors. Perhaps he didn't know what it was like to dance in a circle to the sound of the five-string viola, things that Serafina loved telling me about in detail. Now, on Sundays, he would stay in front of the TV, taking care of the children and waiting for his wife, Eliana, to return from the evangelical services. It was said in the neighborhood that she went to meet Alceu, the butcher. Where else could she get meat with no money? asked Serafina.

Moacir, a bit embarrassed, wanted to know if I could pay my rent ahead of time. He mentioned the medicines he needed to buy for his mother and the kids. The pharmacy is where the poor really get fucked.

I took part of the money I'd got from pawning the watch and paid for the following month. I asked a few questions and, without hearing anything he said, began thinking about whether Moacir might be the person I was looking for, a kind of mule, to operate my clandestine business. He had been in the area for a long time. He knew lots of people. And our proximity would allow me to control the situation.

I asked him if he wanted extra work. Easy money.

If it really *is* easy, he said, with a shrill laugh.

I thought I'd have to use all my telemarketer's glibness to convince the Indian, but when I opened the drawer beside my bed and took out the fifty envelopes, Moacir was already sold. He started to jabber, saying that he himself had thought about going to Puerto Suárez and opening his own business, that it was a waste to have Bolivia practically in our backyard and not to take advantage of it, that he knew a guy there, Juan, who packaged capsules and was a friend of the biggest kingpin, Ramirez, and another, Wilsão, who had taken half a kilo to Araraquara in his stomach, and that "swallowing drugs" brought in "a bundle of dough." Wilsão had been arrested afterward, he said, and that's the problem. Wilsão drank and talked too much. When he asked me if Sulamita would cover for us, I answered yes and no, no and yes; I equivocated. Depends. You have to be discreet, I said, don't say anything to her, leave Sulamita to me.

Before he left, I insisted that he be discreet.

Later I changed my mind and went after Moacir to dissolve the partnership, but he wasn't at home anymore.

Sulamita phoned me when I returned home. The plane had been found in the Paraguay River, and she and Joel had taken part in the recovery.

I should have kept quiet, just waiting. Instead, I got in my van and left. I had learned something: it's while waiting that you start exchanging ideas with the devil, over.

9

Leaving Highway 26A, in the direction of Onça Hill, the stretch of dirt road begins. The air is pleasant and calm, and you smell the fragrance of flowers from the woods. On the radio, the same old thing: music and trash. Luciene and Josias got drunk and smoked grass all Saturday afternoon. After he was caught, Josias confessed that he'd received a demonic order from heaven to dismember the girl as soon as she fell asleep. Since she took a long time to do so, Josias decided to strangle her before cutting her up. The pieces of the girl were thrown into Deep Creek.

I opened the window and repeated, So far so good, over. I'm not Josias, I didn't dismember anyone. I don't know Luciene. I'm not floating in Deep Creek, over.

At the first bridge, a police car followed by an ambulance passed me. I knew very well where they were heading and felt a certain relief. And also fear.

I bypassed the gas station and parked near the restaurant. If that actually was a party, I was the first to arrive.

In the narrow, run-down shed, there wasn't room for ten tables. It was decorated with drawings of ibises, tapirs, parakeets, cormorants, herons, and crows that Carlão himself had painted and that I had nicknamed the Pantanal Horror Show. It had formerly been a restaurant, but now the place sold trinkets to tourists because Rita wasn't a good cook like Carlão's ex-wife.

The kitchen was in the rear, looking out onto a large open patio. I imagined that Rita and Carlão had decided to hold the party outside because of the heat.

I found Rita by herself, seated in a lounge chair, smoking and drinking. She was wearing a light green dress, the skirt raised and crumpled in her lap so that her firm, pretty legs were visible. Her hair, gathered in a knot, formed a kind of nest on top of her head.

You're the first to arrive, she said. You win a prize. A one-way ticket to anywhere a long way from Corumbá.

I sat down in the chair beside her, and she immediately put her feet with their bright-red nails in my lap. She was drunk.

I asked about Carlão and she told me he'd gone for beer. It's gonna be a big party; I even invited a group of guitar players. You like to dance?

I said no.

I'll try to teach you, but it isn't easy. You have to let me lead.

What about the other guests?

They're getting here. Along with the food. I ordered everything. A huge cake like your mother used to make. In layers. And you, you rude man, still haven't congratulated me. How old do you think I am?

Congratulations.

How old?

What?

How old?

I don't know. Not old.

Take a guess, she said, stamping with her foot on my right thigh.

Twenty-two.

Almost. I'm not gonna be specific, 'cause ten years from now I don't want you to know my age.

I removed her legs from my lap, but she put them back again.

I'm never getting old, she said. I use cream all over my face. And if I'm ugly at forty I'll kill myself. I'd rather die young than get all wrinkled. Do you think I'm pretty?

Yes. Where's Carlão?

I'm the one having a birthday, not Carlão. It's about me today.

She got up and pulled me by the hand. Let's have a beer, she said, before the party starts.

In the kitchen, she opened the refrigerator, took out two cans and handed me one. And then she wrapped her arms around my neck. I felt the cold can against the back of my neck, and the chill went down my spine.

What are we doing here? she asked.

The party, I said. Cake, dancing, etc.

I'm talking about our future. A plan for our lives. A project. Why don't we run away from here?

Carlão is taking a long time, I said.

You're not going to tell me you plan to marry a corrupt cop who you hardly know.

She's not corrupt, I said.

But she's a cop. And all cops are corrupt. Let's speak the truth: the vacation was great. You got out of that funk of yours and I had a real good time in the Pantanal. It was cool with Carlão. I mean, until I met you it was cool. But Carlão is an old man.

I started to laugh. Carlão is only three years older than me, I said.

It's exactly those three years that fuck everything up, it's the same difference between a woman of thirty-seven and one of forty, understand? A fundamental difference. I'm not into him anymore. It was cool and all, but I've had enough.

Corumbá is for the birds. You're from São Paulo, and I'm not from here myself. This is no place for the two of us. I know very well that you're crazy about me. From the day you set foot in here I saw how you looked at me. I know why you moved out of here. You don't want to hurt Carlão. But mark my words, the two of us have to be together.

It was only then that she told me that Carlão had gone to Campo Grande. Also, that there wasn't a party at all. And it's not my birthday, she said.

By then she was laughing and kissing me. Until that day, I can honestly say I tried to resist. When things between her and me heated up, I disappeared. And when she called me I wouldn't answer, or if I answered I'd blow her off. And when I began thinking about Rita I remembered the day Carlão had called me into his office and shown me a gun, saying that it was how problems were resolved in those parts.

If the whole thing were just a film, we'd be at the moment when you feel like telling the character to get out of there. It's a tense scene: the character knocks at the door of the fatal house and asks, Anyone there? No one answers and he goes in anyway. And inside there's a killer or a dead body or both. In the film, the guy goes ahead and the rest you know already. Lots of blood. Pure adrenaline. In real life, you don't go in. By way of compensation, you do worse things. You rob a cadaver. You hire some loser of an Indian to sell the blow you stole off the corpse. You fuck your cousin's wife. You do that because you believe you can make a mistake, just one, just one more, and another, just one more little screw-up, and then return and go on with your path, your film, because the course of life continues there, static, waiting for you to screw up and return later.

Before I realized it, we were on the floor, her grunting, me sweating, both of us in a clumsy frenzy like the dogs

I've seen copulating in the vacant lot next to my house. We barely managed to rip our clothes off, we fucked clothed, with Rita's panties chafing my cock. The heat and the fear of being caught increased my desire; I let her take charge, the bitch. On top of me. Lick my face, she said, bite me, suck me, put it in, put it in, deeper, and then, just as I was about to come, she started calling me puppy, and it was as if that word had the power to drag me away and make me understand what was going on. You're gonna be at my feet, puppy, she said, you're gonna obey me, be my slave. I was overcome with terror, Puppy, a collar, she repeated, breaking the rhythm, not allowing me to come, and it was only then that I grasped what was happening and decided to set things straight. I got her off me, placed her on the floor. She opened her legs but I didn't plunge into that fissure. Instead I held her head between my legs and did the rest by myself, using my hands, until I came.

I left her lying there, her face smeared with cum.

10

I drank two cups of coffee.

You don't look very happy, said Dalva when I entered the pantry.

I was late, but no one seemed to care. The atmosphere in the house was completely unlike the day before. There were many people in the garden, friends, politicians, and journalists, and trays with coffee and juice came nonstop from the kitchen. We could even hear a few laughs if we paid attention. Did you hear? Dalva asked.

I already knew everything and repeated to myself: so far so good, over. Everything under control.

Hours earlier I had woken up startled inside the van, with Sulamita leaning against my window. What're you doing here? she asked, giving me a kiss. I had parked in front of her house, waiting for her to return from the rescue mission.

Morning came and we went to the local bakery, holding hands. Sulamita's pants were stained with mud, wet up to the knees. I began talking about my new job right away, emphasizing the name of the family so she would make the inevitable association, and when it happened, I was overcome with an uneasy feeling as if I were stuck in mud. Quite a coincidence, she said.

Afterward, while we were having coffee, she told me that the plane had gotten stuck in a sandbar, with its cabin out of the water, and that it had been recovered and there was a chance the pilot was still alive.

I thought I hadn't heard right.

He wasn't there, she repeated.

Who?

The pilot.

He wasn't in the plane?

His safety belt was undone, and both the plane's doors were unlatched.

She said there was a theory that the youth had lost his memory and was wandering through the woods. Or was seriously injured, somewhere in the nearby area. Two teams, one by land and another by air, were combing the Pantanal at that moment.

She also said that all the investigators had been reassigned to speed up the search. When we have a case like this, she said, it's always the same old story: the governor squeezes the secretary, who squeezes the director, who squeezes the department head, who squeezes the precinct chief, and the thing explodes in the ranks.

Later, at home, in the shower, I had to repeat aloud to myself that there was no way they could involve me in that episode. They couldn't incriminate me. Arrest me. I hadn't done anything. Except steal. I had checked the boy's pulse twice. Very good coke, over. I reviewed everything, every detail, organizing my thoughts. It wasn't hard to imagine what happened after I left the scene of the accident. My mistake was undoing the pilot's safety harness and not closing the doors. It was a lapse on my part. Dead, over. Released, he was carried off by the current. Rotted, over. It was a matter of time, they would find the body caught in some bend of the river. I read somewhere that bacteria work quickly in cases of death. That idea also tormented me: the corpse floating, its face in the mud, the belly swollen, and flies buzzing around it.

On the other hand, there was a degree of comfort in it. So far everything's okay, I told myself. I'm not the cadaver. I'm not going to rot. Or float, over.

For the rest of the morning I stayed in the garage, listening to the news on the radio. The topic was nonstop. They said lots of things. That the open area aided the sweep and that the pilot would be found in the next few hours. That the pilot was a black belt in judo. That he was in excellent physical shape. That he had won the latest equestrian competition in Rio de Janeiro. Rich family. They repeated that a lot, the wealth. All that money, I thought, doesn't keep you from ending up like that. In the swamp. They also said that Junior was a young man much loved by all. Handsome. A good guy. Except they didn't mention that he liked snorting coke. Incredible how a tragedy is enough to turn an ordinary person into a hero.

It was that same day, a bit later, that I saw her for the first time. Dona Lu, that's what everybody called her. Lu for Lourdes.

She was under fifty, compact, and seemed to be made of some material that would break easily. The type of person who, if I were God, I'd pay to play on my team. She looked you in the eye when she spoke, without affectation, in a very feminine way. I don't know how to deal with that type. The result of certain combinations, wealth with kindness, beauty with kindness, wealth with beauty, or even just kindness or pure beauty is very destructive. It puts an end to you. You're reduced to dust, that's the truth.

Dona Lu stood beside the car, waiting for me to open the door. The subtle smell of a rich woman quickly permeated everything. It took me a time to understand that my duties also included opening doors.

She asked me to take her to the church. On the way she asked several questions: if I was married, if I had children, family, if I liked Corumbá. She also said that I had brought good luck to her family. And that the police thought her son was still alive. She herself was certain of it. You'll like him, she said.

She also asked if I was religious. I remembered reading somewhere that people prefer celebrities to Santa Claus. Actresses, in my opinion, are more interesting than saints. Between Madonna and Hail Mary I would stick with Madonna, but you can't say that in surveys or to Dona Lu.

There was no one in the church. Just coolness and the dim light and her, on her knees, praying. I felt sorry for her, felt like shortening the path she would have to follow. I thought that if I told her the boy was dead, if I took her to see the body and she could give him a proper burial, with a wake and flowers, if she could cry at the tomb, she wouldn't, like my mother, have to keep the home fires burning for a long time. Stark death isn't the hardest thing. Worse is mystery. Doubt. That's what destroys us.

We went home in silence, and in the rearview mirror I saw that Dona Lu was crying softly.

That devastated me. I remembered my mother crying, the tears dripping into the beaten egg whites. I thought about the happy brides who ate my mother's cakes of tears at their wedding parties.

That night, I went to pick up Sulamita at the precinct. There was a farewell party; it was her last day on the job. The next day she would be transferred to the Forensics division, as head of the morgue.

They were drinking beer, sitting at the tables.

Know what her work's gonna be? they asked me.

I had no idea. They laughed, trying to tease me.

Sulamita's gonna talk with cadavers, they said. Laughter. Now it's serious, they told me. A corpse is the plane's black box. Everything's recorded in that hunk of flesh, and you just have to sit down and know how to listen. The deceased. The dead truly speak. They tell all. Who did it. How he did it. That's how you crack the crime, they said. Someone added, My best teachers were the great killers. The hard part, they said, is putting up with the smell.

A young guy I'd never seen there, with thin legs and a voluminous belly, recalled an investigation in which the detective, new at the time, and who later died of a heart attack, went into the bathroom in the victim's house, got some perfume and scattered it around the place. Just imagine the smell. Rotting flesh with perfume. They guffawed. The stench, said the precinct chief, whose name was Pedro Caleiro, that hot smell of rot along with the perfume – I almost killed Raul, the idiot. We were sweating like pigs. They laughed loudly. Especially Dudu, the chief's assistant, a blond guy with blue eyes and the face of an old Weimaraner. It was he who suggested that Sulamita use Vicks VapoRub.

It was a hot night, suffocating. I stopped paying attention to what they were saying. The image of Dona Lu weeping behind her sunglasses wouldn't leave my head.

What's wrong? Sulamita asked.

I must've drunk too much, I said, and went out to vomit in the hallway, where a few tires and other junk were blocking the exit.

Sulamita brought a glass of soda. She sat down by me and took my hand. Are you feeling any better?

I said yes.

She said her family wanted to meet me. My mother's going to make lunch for you on Sunday.

I asked if she would mind if I left.

Sulamita was affectionate with me. I'll take you to the car, she said.

As I was leaving, I heard her ask Joel, Can you give me a ride, Tranqueira?

Of course, Sweetheart.

At home, I kept tossing in bed, looking at the clock, unable to sleep. The image of the body floating in the river wouldn't leave my mind.

At three o'clock I got up, went to the pay phone at the corner and called the Beraba family.

I have some important information, I told whoever answered the phone.

Who's calling?

I recognized the rancher's voice.

Your son is dead, I said.

And hung up.

11

First Brian blew his brains out. Ten days later, Robbie hanged himself. And then Justin drank rat poison. And Max, three days later, followed the path of Brian, Robbie, and Justin. I thought to myself, the people in that area, Texas, I'm not sure exactly where it was, Wisconsin, the people there must wake up every morning wondering who's going to hang himself today. Who's going to jump from the tenth floor?

It's no coincidence, concluded the experts. I don't know where I read the story, but the theory is that it's an epidemic. Somebody kills himself and the news spreads like the flu. A powerful virus. It appears in all the papers, on television, radio, and those dead who hours before were just a shy student, just a widower, a peaceful appliance salesman, or the son of Chinese immigrants, with no talent or luster, are transformed into celebrities like movie actors or baseball players. A dark fame, true. Infectious stars.

The others, the ones who don't kill themselves, foster death and mount the spectacle. That's also part of the sickness. They gossip, comment, really smear themselves. They devour newspapers. They live off that. The funeral is a great event, with the presence of the mayor, who eulogizes the hanged man in a lovely speech. Schoolchildren join hands and sing a hymn. A period of mourning is declared and the team flag is flown at half-staff. It's like the awarding of a local Oscar. It's a prize, the homage. You kill yourself, and in exchange you become famous in your little town. For a few days. And sometime later, somebody else hangs himself, and then another, in a vicious circle that paradoxically lends life to those dead cities with names like Frostproof.

An epidemic, say the sociologists. And it does no good to wash your hands. No good to disinfect with alcohol. Or wear a mask. The only way for you not to blow your brains out is to turn off the television. Turn off the radio. Not to read newspapers. To leave the city.

I felt contaminated myself. In my opinion, what we were experiencing in Corumbá was an outbreak. Of a different sort, but equally vicious. In all the papers, on the radio and television, the exclusive topic was the pilot's accident. The difference was that no one had killed himself. It was pitiful seeing Dona Lu. She had lost a lot of weight. I practically had to carry her to the car when we went to the church. On those occasions, the vultures hovered around her, all but asking for autographs. Does it hurt badly? is what they wanted to know. How much does it hurt to have a son disappear? Jackals after raw meat. They liked feeling pity for that rich and attractive woman, who was royally screwed despite being rich and attractive. They felt good about that. Dona Lu's misfortune allowed them to feel sympathetic. In fact, that's another symptom of the epidemic. Pathological generosity that surges in the community. Instead of fever and diarrhea, there suddenly appears that symptom, compassion.

The young people of the city organized and went out in search of the pilot, in the vicinity of the Old Highway. At the location of the accident there was now a cross. And flowers. JUNIOR LIVES. Banners like that proliferated around the city.

The worst part was the vigils. I would sometimes arrive for work and there was no other way to get into the garage except by stepping on flowers and candles. We would gather up the bouquets to open a path, throw everything in the trash, but right away they would bring more flowers, more garbage, and block the entrance again. On a Monday, there were also bags of French fries and Coca-Cola cans strewn around. In the riding area. Where people suffered a little to enjoy themselves a lot. At the misfortune of others. Instead of going to the park or the movies, they suffered on our sidewalk, joining hands, with prayer and song. And later, tired of amusing themselves by crying, they would return to their homes, satiated.

There was no rest. By day, indignation, and at night, bad dreams. In them there was always a cake with several layers, like the ones my mother used to make, and on top, instead of the smiling bride and groom, was the wreckage of an airplane around which vultures and gulls circled endlessly. I observed the small dark cloud of birds and, as I was getting up to shoo them away, I realized I was moving with the vultures. I woke up, feeling the giddiness of rapture. Or of falling, I don't really remember.

The epidemic didn't last long. A month, perhaps. A bit more. And when we were at the apex, with the entire city greatly enjoying itself, the inevitable happened. That's how an epidemic works, according to immunologists. It peaks and then begins to retreat. Descend. Really plummet.

Just as we were beginning to experience a bit of peace, Dona Lu sank for good. She wasn't resigned. How could my son, so loved, my only son, my love, not come through this door again? I want my son, she repeated to her husband like a spoiled little girl.

We could hear her sobs from the kitchen. Doctors came to sedate her. But she would wake up and resume her wailing. Sometimes she would become confused and ask us if

Junior had woken up, if he'd had breakfast. Sometimes she would call me to look at albums of Junior as a child. We spent afternoons like that, looking at photos from the past.

I recall that one day when I returned from the bank where I'd gone to pay some bills, I went to look for her in the office to give her the receipts and found her with her head on the desk, weeping uncontrollably, crying like a small child. Where is my son? she asked when I came in. I want my son, she said, almost imploring, looking into my eyes, that's how she spoke to people, with her penetrating gaze, fearless, and when you answered, she would listen with almost childish attention, believing, as if the others were incapable of lying.

What could I say at that moment? That her son was food for the piranhas?

True, I had said that. In different form. Not to her, to her husband. If she answered the phone I hung up. But on two occasions, in the middle of the night, from the pay phone at the corner of my block, when I was sure it was him on the phone, I said point-blank: your son is dead.

And hung up. I thought the information would help, that knowing it they would go forward, look for the body in the river or else start to accept the idea that their son had died, at least that, but what's odd is that at no time did they take that hypothesis into consideration. Some crazy guy keeps calling, Dalva said one morning. A psychopath.

And so my warnings were just one more element of the family's nightmare. They would listen to me and the next day go on believing their son would be found. They didn't want to know that he had fallen into a river full of piranhas. They didn't even give it a thought. The piranhas. They had raised cattle for decades and were all too familiar with losing steers to the piranhas in the very river where their son had crashed, but they chose to overlook that detail.

Five weeks after the accident I received my first pay and took Sulamita for pizza in a restaurant near the belvedere on Santo Inácio Hill, from which we could see a stretch of the Paraguay River in the distance.

The night was hot, stuffy, and we sat at a table outside to enjoy the view.

Sulamita was a bit down, and I felt her mood had to do with my reluctance to meet her family. She had been insisting on it for some weeks, and I had put her off a little because of Rita. Not that I didn't like Sulamita. But Rita was something else entirely. Rita was as bubbly as a waterfall, everything about her was lushness and strength, hyper-feminine, legs exposed, always wearing rings, necklaces, and clogs, always gesticulating. I was crazy about all of it.

Carlão believed she was attending to clients, and Sulamita thought I was putting in overtime at the Berabas', and we would go to motels, fill the tub and stay there, fucking and escaping the heat.

One day we were embracing in bed after making love when I asked why she didn't get out if her relationship with Carlão was so bad. I think that at the time I was also thinking about a more serious step with Rita. Why? she said. Because I have a heart. Carlão left a long-standing marriage and two daughters to be with me, and now that I'm with you, in a good thing, now that I'm in love with you I just say ciao? Just like that? No, I'm not that kind of woman. I want to do things right, she said. Without hurting anybody.

After that, I understood where Rita was coming from and slowed things down. Actually, I saw it was time to end the affair. But that wasn't easy. We had a crazy connection, she knew how to keep me close. Naturally, we started fighting a lot too. Especially because of Sulamita. Or Carlão. I didn't like the idea of dumping Sulamita, and that irritated Rita.

Carlão also exasperated me. He would sometimes call three times in a row to ask dumb questions. A goddamn drag. You're not even married and already act like a husband, she said. That's when things heated up. We'd fight, she'd phone and I wouldn't answer, or vice versa. I would plead, she would plead, we'd both say no and yes, yes and no, we'd make up and then fight again, go back, and get offended, then make up again.

Our relationship really heated up one Thursday when I went out to have some beers with Carlão and he told me he wanted to have a child with Rita. I got pissed off.

That Saturday at the pizzeria, in that infernal heat, without even the hint of a breeze, I finally told Sulamita she could set up the lunch with her family on Sunday.

She kissed me and said she loved me. But she was still sad, I noticed. Sad and in love.

On Sunday I woke up resolved to get my life back in order. Rita called and I made a point of telling her, I'm going to meet Sulamita's family, and we may get engaged. You're ridiculous, she answered, and hung up in my face, before I could tell her she was the one who was ridiculous with that talk about a baby.

As I was getting ready to leave, Moacir knocked at the door. I had been trying to talk with him for a week, to find out what the fuck was going on, why he was so tuned out, didn't open his workshop anymore, slept late, left the junk piled up at the entrance to the house, cans from the shop. The neighborhood kids were already starting to steal that crap.

He was also drinking. At least that's what Sulamita kept telling me. But what really worried me was Eliana. It was true that we were making some money. Not much, because my strategy was to sell cheaply to undercut the competition. But it was dribs and drabs, coming in every day. Every day

Moacir would push a few fives and tens under the door of my room: he paid for his part, and that was good for both of us, I could spend it all without calling attention, I spent it on motels and restaurants with Rita, and with Sulamita too, I'd bought a ring for Sulamita that I was going to take to the lunch, and a tray for Sulamita's mother and a hunting knife for her father. I spent everything, but without calling attention to myself, while Moacir – what a bungler, and that business of not opening the workshop? And Eliana, who went around in new clothes, all dolled up? Why'd she dyed her hair blonde? To make herself stand out?

On Friday, as I was leaving for work, I noticed that everybody in Moacir's house, including Serafina, was wearing new sneakers. The same model. What's this, I asked, a football team? I explained to Moacir that he was attracting unwanted attention. You think the people in the neighborhood don't see it? You go barefoot and all of a sudden show up in new Reeboks? You think people don't spot the splurge?

I'll be careful, he said. He swore he'd talk to Eliana, but I noticed that he reeked of alcohol, and became more concerned.

I'm talking seriously, I said.

I know, Moacir answered. He asked how much of the drug we had left.

A little less than two hundred grams, I answered.

Is that all? We don't even need to bag it. Let me have it all, I have a major buyer.

The sun was searing when I got in the car, and the land-scape shimmered like it was a bad film.

12

Your car was stolen? Go to Puerto Suárez and see if it's there. That's what I'd read about the city. Now I was driving through the muddy streets of Puerto Suárez, though my van hadn't been stolen. We were there, Moacir and me, to negotiate.

Ever since our supply ran out, Moacir wouldn't leave me alone. He stopped drinking, got his act together, and when he hammered his old pieces of junk in his hot, dirty workshop, he would try to convince me to meet his friend Ramirez, the Bolivian. Or rather, almost friend. I'm friends with a guy who works for him, Moacir had said. Juan. Another Bolivian. Their scheme is foolproof, you just have to use your own car.

The more I resisted, the more Moacir tried to convince me. With a van like mine, he said, I'd be rolling in dough. Know what my plan is?

He was funny, with those stripped bikes in that shithole shack, the Indian was talking about the future. *My* plan is to get away, I said, to get the hell out. We'll make a bundle with Ramirez, he promised. Ramirez's like you, he don't want problems. He wants money. You and him got a lot in common, you know? You're gonna be friends, I'm sure of it. Ramirez only gets along with people like you. If everything works out and we get in, know what I wanna do with my part? Open up a real workshop, with a gigantic hydraulic lift, you know, a hydraulic jack? To raise the car? Right in downtown

Corumbá. Hire a couple of guys to work with me. Everybody in uniforms. If you go to Puerto Suárez with me and meet Ramirez, you'll see how easy it is to get the dough.

Naturally, I didn't take any of that seriously. In reality, it was Sulamita's reaction the next day when she discovered Rita's panties in my bedroom that made me change my mind. Whose are they? she asked. I don't know, I answered, preparing for a fight that never came. Actually, what happened between us was anticlimactic. First a great silence, then an emptiness, a void. Sulamita said nothing, and I started to make up things while she sat on the edge of the bed, under control, biting her lip, listening to me repeat that I didn't know how the panties had got there, I swear I don't know, I repeated, it must be something the Indians did, those goddamn kids, they come into houses, rummage around in everything – and then Sulamita interrupted and said that whenever she received a body in the morgue she couldn't help thinking that hours before that piece of meat was breathing, the heart beating, the blood flowing. It hurt to think, she said, that he, the cadaver, had plans before he died, a trip, a house, a child, forgiveness, whatever, you always think you can put off your dream till tomorrow, you think "I'll take care of it tomorrow," but then you catch a bullet in the brain, or die run over by a truck, or your heart bursts, and just like that it's all over. There *is* no tomorrow. She said this the Sunday I met her parents, while we were eating the fish her mother had spent all morning preparing, all of us at the table. She could hardly breathe from such happiness. Finally, she said, I thought I had found the man who would be the father of my children. That was me. Project Children, of course. Me, the father. The provider. Full of responsibilities. Suddenly, she continued, I could see a wonderful future for me and my family. That was my dream, right in front of me, and I thought we would make it come true. The dream. You and I. The fact that her father, her mother, and her sister liked me only served to confirm her dream. We were going to save our money, she said, and buy some land in the Pantanal. Build a house. Raise cattle. And now, she said, those panties, those stinking panties from some vulgar woman, have ended it all.

Sulamita wasn't nasty or accusatory. She was sad, vulnerable, and for that reason her dream hit me hard that night; I could almost taste blood in my mouth. Raise cattle in the Pantanal, a family. I imagined ourselves like Dona Lu and José Beraba, without the dead son, of course, but the same kind of solid marriage, the kind only money can sustain, businesses, cattle, a future as certain as a mathematical formula, and I was thinking about that when I kneeled beside Sulamita and set the panties on fire with my lighter, swearing to never again do anything that might hurt her, nothing, I said, and asked her to forgive me, said that I wanted the same thing she did, marriage, land, children, whatever you decide is fine with me.

A man can't spend the rest of his life screwing around with crazy women like Rita.

Sulamita and I made love that night in a different way, without fury or anxiety like with Rita, much less our usual way, eager and affectionate, it was something deep, throbbing, impulsive. I plunged toward something very profound, deep down, a grotto, and returned to the surface moaning, happy, plunged and submerged, very slowly and with great impetus, advancing and retreating, until I came.

The next day I went to Moacir and said, Let's go ahead with that project.

We don't have any money, Moacir had explained, so it's ideal for us. 'Cause Ramirez doesn't want customers. He wants partners.

I made it quite clear that this would be the one and only time I would get involved in anything like that. But don't say that to Juan, he said. We take the money and get out. I don't wanna fuck up my life either. I'm gonna set up a real cool workshop, that's all I want.

I spoke to Sulamita too, lying that I had some money set aside. We'll pool our savings and buy a small piece of land. A beginning, over.

Now, walking down the pitted streets of Puerto Suárez, we looked for the bar where Juan, Ramirez's friend, would be waiting for us. I had called Dalva and said I wouldn't be working that day because I had diarrhea. Dalva told me about a remedy using water and cornstarch. Use it and tomorrow you'll be fine.

How is she? I asked.

Dona Lu? Very bad, Dalva replied.

I hung up the phone with a sadness in my breast. I truly wanted Dona Lu to heal, and told Dalva so. But think about it, she answered. How do you heal from the death of a son?

We drank a soda; the owner of the bar had the radio tuned to a Brazilian station, hearing news from Brazil and commercials for Brazilian products. I listened and thought there must not be a worse punishment in the world than to be born in Puerto Suárez.

Ten minutes later, Juan came into the bar wearing a hat and a red shirt. Let's take your car, he said.

We got into the van. So far, I told myself, so good, over. Juan was a likable guy and enjoyed speaking Portuguese. Turn left, then straight ahead, he said. Actually, his Portuguese was as rotten as my Spanish, and if he thought he was speaking Portuguese, I also believed I was communicating in Spanish. Take another left, he said. And then he asked if I liked *puerco*. I answered yes, mucho. They make a magnificent roast *puerco*

59

here, pointing to a bar that had nothing magnificent about it. To the right and then to the left, he said.

Then Juan began explaining how he had learned Portuguese, from watching telenovelas, he said, another left, and that's how I learned, to the left now, but I also take chances, like the case of *puerco*. I didn't know how to say *puerco* in Portuguese, he said, but I deduced it was like in Spanish: *puerco*.

It's not *puerco*, it's *porco*, I said.

No? he said, laughing. Do I talk that bad? From then on, he started calling me Porco. Porco this, Porco that: what could I do?

Moacir didn't participate in the conversation, he just looked out the window, absorbed like a child being carried by his parents.

We were leaving the city when Juan told me to park, pointing to a house with unplastered walls. The district was even poorer and more desolate than downtown, and it afforded a clear view of the area. Two young men, shirtless and armed, were the security for the place.

We were taken inside the dwelling, crossed the living room, where a couple, seated ceremoniously on a dilapidated sofa, were taken aback by our presence. We went through the kitchen, toward the rear of the house, until we came to a spacious backyard, cemented and partially covered. Ramirez was there, beside a compressing machine, overseeing the job of compacting the pasty base. I was introduced as Porco, Moacir's friend. Now it was official, I thought. Porco. You're gonna have to wait a little, Juan said. I just need the car keys.

I didn't like that, but Moacir stepped up, took the key from my hand, and handed it to a young guy who had just arrived and was beside Juan.

We watched as Ramirez skillfully packaged the drug. Strips of fine transparent backing paper were placed in the holes of the press. Using a spoon, he adjusted the drug on the plastic and then sealed the capsules with a nylon thread.

As we watched, the side gate opened and my van came through, driven by the youth who had taken the key minutes earlier.

Two more young men came from the house and began talking with the driver about the best place to hide the drugs. I felt uneasy. What's going on? I asked Moacir. Take it easy, he said. Everything's cool.

At that moment the couple who were in the living room when we arrived joined us, each carrying a bottle of water. I finally understood what those poor devils, neophytes like us, were doing there. Ramirez gave the instructions, and in the next twenty minutes the couple swallowed a large number of capsules, close to 800 grams of the drug. The narcotic would be transported inside their bodies, that same day, to somewhere in southern Brazil.

The woman looked like a frightened rodent about to be hunted. I thought she would faint at any moment.

Juan left, taking the couple with him, and only then did Ramirez start talking to us.

By then, the exhaust pipe had already been removed from my van. I was panic-stricken when I realized what the scheme was: we would be taking ten kilos of coke, and not two as I had agreed with Moacir. Five would be picked up by another agent of Ramirez's the next day, and the rest was ours. For our work, we would get forty days to settle our debt.

I took Moacir aside. Have you gone mad? I asked. That's not what we agreed.

Stay cool, he said. Everything's okay.

I panicked.

I went into the bathroom, my urge was to dump Moacir and the van right there, and then Moacir came after me and said, You think I'd put everybody, Eliana, my kids, my mother, at risk? Think I'm crazy? Trust me, he said. It's gonna work out.

When Ramirez explained to us how crossing the border would be, I thought he had to be joking. It's just that, Ramirez said, the less you two know, the better. Stay calm. Cross the border like it isn't nothing.

What if they stop us? Arrest us?

None of that's gonna happen, Moacir said. Ramirez guarantees it.

On the trip back, I was trembling from head to toe. You don't have the slightest notion of what we're doing, I told Moacir, you're a nutcase, clueless, in your tribe there's nothing like this, you think you're clever but you're nothing but a clueless Indian. He laughed, calmly. Look at Juan there, he said, pointing, when we were about to cross the border, he's gonna help us. I saw Juan parking the car, from which the terrified rodent and the young man with their bellies stuffed with drugs got out. Juan fled.

We were about to pass by the guards when the two unfortunates practically cut us off. And then seven cops, along with those in the guard post, appeared and surrounded the couple, who were handcuffed and dragged off somewhere.

As for us, we weren't even searched. A piece of cake. Seeing the two of them screwed.

As soon as we were at a safe distance, I stopped the car. You stupid Indian, I yelled, feeling my legs shaking.

Everything's been all right from the beginning, said Moacir. I knew.

Knew what?

Ramirez and Juan ratted out the couple. They do that, it's normal. They turned them in so we could get through.

You fucker, I said. You knew?

I started the car. You shitass Indian, I said. You're not worth a damn.

On the rest of the way, I didn't even look at Moacir. He started telling a long story, how Ramirez had five brothers, and that he knew the second oldest, and how one of them was in prison. Shut up, I said, you're making me even more nervous.

13

What are you doing here? Sulamita asked as soon as I entered the morgue. I had the feeling that she didn't want me to kiss her.

Sulamita had asked me several times not to go there, not even to pick her up after work. That place isn't like a precinct, she had said, or a government office. Sometimes I feel like I'm in the devil's kitchen. And that's where I work. Where the devil cooks up misfortune. We have a huge refrigerator, rusty, and every morning my heart races when I think of what I'm going to find in those drawers. You can't imagine the smell that impregnates our clothes and hair. The smell of carrion, sulfur, garbage. Think of any kind of stench you're familiar with, it's worse there, she had said. It's rancid and thick, you can almost pick it up with your hands. I don't want you to visit me. Not you, not anyone.

I didn't think about any of that when I went to get her. I had phoned twice, but apparently answering calls wasn't the morgue's forte. My head was boiling, I tried to calm down, I needed a bit of the comfort that Sulamita's mere presence brought me, and that's why I was there.

An hour earlier, I'd been in bed listening to Moacir dismantling my car in his workshop, nervous because I knew ten kilos of cocaine were there, when Rita knocked at the door. In shorts, boots, with braids in her hair. She couldn't have chosen a worse moment, I thought. Smoking. Enormous gall on her part. Rita was incredible. She wanted to know what "weird business" was "going down" between us. Why didn't I answer my cell phone? What had she done wrong? Didn't I love her anymore?

Rita was a cynic. Her breasts free under her T-shirt and her nails painted a garish orange, as if she wanted to catch me in a snare.

Carlão told me you're pregnant, I said. I know everything. The baby you two are having. A beautiful family, I said. I can't understand how you can do that to Carlão. Pregnant and coming here after me. I also said she disgusted me. It's one thing, Rita, for us to have some fun, another for you to have a child with Carlão.

The child is yours, she replied. Just like that, to my face. And then she explained, confusedly, that she really had talked with Carlão even before speaking with me, despite the child being mine and not his. It's yours, she said over and over, not his, it's really yours, I was just preparing the ground. You know it's not his, but Carlão is a great guy, it's yours, and you remember how Carlão helped you when you were all screwed up? When that telemarketer woman killed herself because of you? I don't want to hurt Carlão, she said. She said: We don't need to do that to people. Goading. Sulamita doesn't deserve to suffer either. That's how I am, I don't like to make anyone suffer. And lately, she concluded, we've fought so much, I don't know what's happening, it's like there's a black cloud hovering over us. You don't answer my phone calls, I didn't have the chance to talk about the pregnancy.

I pushed Rita away, I don't believe it, I said, get out and leave me alone, and that was when she grabbed my arm, shouting that the child was mine. You idiot, she said, you idiotic piece of shit, whose do you think it is? I was afraid the neighbors would hear.

65

Lower your voice, goddammit.

The child is yours. Get that through your skull. I'm one month pregnant. And now you want to run away from your responsibility? You think you can get me pregnant and just run away?

We fell silent, lost in thought, at the door to my bedroom. Down below, Moacir was still hammering my car.

How can I be sure you're not lying?

She laughed wearily.

I'm not joking, I said. You lie so often to Carlão. In fact, what guarantee is there that the child isn't Carlão's? Or whoever's? How many men do you have, Rita?

And then Rita slapped me; at the time, I remembered my telemarketer who'd committed suicide. It's not everyone who's up to taking a slap like that. I'm going to tell you the truth, Rita said, the child isn't yours. I'd never have a child with a fool like you.

I wasn't prepared for that upside-down declaration. I watched Rita leave, coldly, descending the stairs in fury. I didn't know whether I should shout, run after her and grab her by the hair, whether I should slam the door with all my strength. My desire was to attack and to ask forgiveness at the same time. To strike and retreat. That was why I went looking for Sulamita.

Did I do the wrong thing coming here? I asked.

I tried to hug her but she drew back.

What is it?

That curse. I already explained it to you, she said. A strange odor impregnates me when I'm here. Can you smell it?

The smell of shampoo, I said, after sniffing her hair.

Really?

Of course. You smell as good as ever, I insisted. But it was a lie. A putrid and nauseating odor came from everywhere, including from Sulamita.

She smiled. Want to see something?

She took me by the hand and led me to the inner chamber of the morgue, an immense room lined with tiles that once had been white but now were merely dingy. In the middle, three ruined stainless-steel tables. On one of them was a cadaver, underneath a sheet that covered almost everything except the feet.

Sulamita explained that the autopsies were done there. Rapes, homicides, a little of everything, she said. People from around here and throughout the region. We get bodies in every day. It's rare for us to have a day, one lousy day, without someone arriving here.

She told me that was her job. Coordinating the autopsy team. Receiving the cadavers, storing them, cleaning them, placing them on the table for the coroner to examine. She also said that she witnessed the autopsies.

And without my asking, she took me to the middle table and pulled back the sheet from the body of a still young woman whose legs were covered with abrasions. A heart-shaped earring was on her right ear.

This one died yesterday, she said.

I noticed that Sulamita was pale.

Rape followed by murder, she continued. They found her tossed into a garbage dump.

We stared at the cadaver for several seconds.

Are you sure, she asked, that I don't have that smell on me?

Yes, I replied, taking her in my arms.

14

Then Sulamita started to cry. I can't go on anymore, she said, I can't take it, I can't and I won't, she repeated endlessly. She sounded like a broken record. I need to go away, she said. I can't take it anymore. She said that when she heard the sound of the meat wagon parking outside, her heart leaped like a toad fleeing from a snake. I can't take it. I feel like I'm going to vomit up my own stomach. I can't go on. Head of the morgue, she said. You know what my function is? It wasn't till the day I signed in and read the job description that I realized what was about to happen to my life. Till then I thought it was some kind of promotion, that I'd stop being an administrative assistant doing bureaucratic work, and make more money. I didn't understand that I'd be working in this horrible world of people who stink and rot. Of course I knew what it was, I took the qualifying exams, studied, knew the names of everything, all the instruments we use, all the types of brushes and clamps and saws that cut through the skull, I knew it all, the technical terms, the procedures, I knew but I didn't understand what they would mean in my life. That rancidity. You smell it, don't you?

And she began to cry again, pressing her hands against her face.

I took Sulamita by the arm. Let's get out of here, I said.

We crossed the street, went into a bar where the families of the cadavers crowded together to eat a cold sandwich while waiting to identify their dead. Everything here's like that, she said, contaminated, there's no place to escape, you can't have a cup of coffee in peace without running into those wretches suffering because their son, their mother, their brother died. Yesterday, a mother who lost her two-year-old son, drowned in the pool, beat her head against the wall and screamed.

I thought about how my own mother would have been happy if one day someone from the morgue had called, if we had gone there, identified my father's body so that later we could bury him and be done with the matter. That's the meaning of the word bury. To put a full stop to something. Bury the dead and take care of the living – who said that? Until we bury the dead, the living stay behind and bleed. The dead destroy us. Destroy Dona Lu. I had noticed that in the last few days it no longer mattered if she found her son alive. Finding his body would be enough. She was at the point where the cadaver was better than nothing. Better the cadaver. It was exactly how things worked. I knew this from my own experience. There are times when even bad news is welcome. We found an arm. A piece of the skull. We caught the killer. The grave. Anything will do.

We ordered Coca-Cola, and Sulamita began repeating that she felt ill from that smell of decomposition, of rotting things, and for me not to come close, my hair stinks, my clothing, the odor sticks like chewing gum, it doesn't do any good to bathe with just soap, she said, if I don't use alcohol on my entire body the smell won't go away.

I tried to calm her, while I tried to calm myself, by speaking of our plans, the land we would buy. I said that soon she'd be able to resign from that place and be free of that stench. So you do smell it? she asked. No, I said. Of course I did, and in fact it was unbearable, a mixture of formaldehyde and offal, with the sun overhead cooking it all.

As long as the two of us aren't able to support my father, my mother, and my sister, I can't leave here, she said. They depend on me. Things were more complicated than I thought. Father, mother, and sister make up a total hell, I thought, and even so I went ahead with my lie, said that ranchers, cattle raisers, farmers also had families, naturally we're going to be able to support ours. Ours, I said, as if it were mine too. Though it was hers. Only hers. When we buy our land, I said, you'll leave all that behind. We're going to have cattle, we're going to make money.

I was certain none of that would happen, but I felt so sorry for Sulamita and so much affection for her that I went on making promises. Anyone overhearing me would believe I didn't think about Rita anymore, though I couldn't get her out of my head for even a second.

I've tried, she said, not looking at the faces of the cadavers. That was the tip they gave me when I got here. Don't look.

I remembered the pilot, his eyes. At times, for no reason, those eyes appeared in my memory. And the final breath. When I took Dona Lu to the church, I also remembered those eyes. The eyes of someone about to die. The eyes die first, that's my impression. Before anything else. They cloud over. And fade away.

Sulamita continued: They said, "Look at the lesion in the liver, the lesion in the stomach, look at the fracture in the skull, look at the lesion, just the lesion." But who says I can do that? I go directly to the eyes. To the face. I can't help it, every day when I come here I tell myself "Today, you idiot, you're not going to see anyone's face." I get here and before I realize it, I'm staring at the face of the deceased. It's like I even want to see that dead face. Like I enjoy seeing it. But I detest it. One more, I think, one more for my funereal gallery. I know very well what the mouth, the nose are like. As soon as I close my eyes the faces parade before me like some horror film.

After ordering coffee, which was lukewarm and tasted of leftover grounds, she told me that part of her job was also assisting at exhumations. They dig up the cadaver and I have to stand there, watching. It's like that here. One task worse than the other. I have to do the sutures after they're all eviscerated. Besides describing the clothes they're wearing, the color of their hair, eyes, teeth. And that's not the worst part. The worst is at night, in bed, having to close my eyes and sleep. That's the worst part. And then wake up and come back here. That's what's terrible.

Last night, she said, the table, which isn't ergonomic because the state can't even get that right, the state doesn't give a shit about its dead, the table twisted as we were carrying an old man who had died of a heart attack, and he rolled onto the floor. I started crying and thought, It's not enough that the man has died, do I also have to drop him?

We remained in the bar for a time; it was almost five o'clock and the sun continued strong, as if it were still early afternoon. I commented on that to Sulamita, and she added, True, that's another problem with my job. Everything in this city rots more quickly.

Out of the way, said Sulamita's mother, coming to the table carrying the steaming platter. Fish with annatto was the dish. My mother-in-law's specialty. I've already tried making broth of piranha and alligator meat, but this is my strong point, the old lady repeated.

It was Sunday and we had spent the morning fishing, my father-in-law and I. En route, we left Sulamita and Regina at the grotto near the Vista Alegre ranch, helped Sulamita take Regina from her wheelchair and place her in the water, then continued ahead to fish.

It was the rainy season, the river was high, its level had risen significantly, forming a body of water that stretched out of sight. Further on in, my father-in-law said, it's real beautiful, there's bayous, swamp birds, lowlands, mountain ranges, salt marshes, one of these days I'll take you there. To me, if God exists he's the Pantanal. We've got everything, we've got forests, we've got pastures, we've got clear fields, we've got the most beautiful birds you can imagine. Today I'm going to teach you to fish, he said. I already knew how to fish, I knew that entire area, I'd hiked through it with Rita, one of our favorite activities. We would sometimes rent a boat and turn off the motor in mid-river and stay there, letting life drift by. Just Rita and me.

Father-in-law, that's what I called him, and he called me my son. To me, he said while we fished, now you're my son. And then he began praising Sulamita: You don't know how precious that woman is, precious and brave. The adjectives poured out like a waterfall. Now she's playing with Regina, who loves to swim. It's only when she's swimming that Regina feels that her legs aren't a hindrance, he said. In the wheelchair she's just a trunk, but in the water her legs are reborn, I think. Sulamita has more patience than you can imagine. Sulamita has a great heart. It wasn't easy for us, he continued, for me and my wife, to have Regina. A crippled child is almost a half-child. A burden for us, and

I say that with total love. At first, her mother didn't even want to look at the girl: she thought she'd given birth to a monster. But Sulamita, who was a little five-year-old girl, gave us a true lesson of love. She was the one who first fell in love with Regina. The older Regina got, the more twisted and ugly she became, but Sulamita loved her. Have you seen how the two get along?

I had seen, and I even forced myself to talk to Regina, though I couldn't understand her grunts. She's saying she wants ice cream, Sulamita would translate, when the three of us went out together. She's saying she wants juice. She's asking me to change her diaper. Sulamita, and only Sulamita, understood that language, which was as twisted and deformed as her sister's body.

After fishing, we went for Sulamita and Regina at the lake. Regina was exhausted and fell asleep in the car on the way back.

Now, ravenous, we sat around the table, along with two of Sulamita's cousins, a widowed aunt, another widowed aunt, and her ninety-year-old grandmother. How chic, said the aunt when Sulamita showed her the ring I had given her. It wasn't an engagement ring, but now it might as well have been. Sulamita herself said it was for an engagement. An elegant thing, the aunt repeated. Really chic, the other aunt said. I had also brought Serafina, explaining that she was like a mother to me, and the Indian woman remained silent, eating nonstop, eating and looking, without understanding anything that was happening.

Sulamita had suggested we invite Carlão and Rita also so she could meet them, but I made up a long story that Rita was having problems of nausea because of the pregnancy. I didn't want to lay eyes on that tramp's face. The gall. Wearing boots and her hand on her hip, wanting to know what was "going down" between us. Shit is going down, I should have answered.

After that day at the morgue, Sulamita and I decided to speed up our plans. Or rather, Sulamita decided. We'd buy a small piece of land and get married. She wanted to get married first, but I was like a bad driver. Forward and backward. More backward than forward. I balked. I hindered the flow. Sometimes I would get really worked up. I even mentioned the marriage to Dona Lu one afternoon when I took her to the doctor. Nowadays she was constantly seeing doctors because she couldn't sleep anymore except with pills. I'm very happy for you, Dona Lu said. I so wanted my son to marry Daniela, but Junior didn't think about serious commitments. A naughty boy. She asked me to inform her when we set a date. We want to give you and your fiancée a gift. We think a lot of you. My husband and I, and Dalva too. You're overqualified for the position of driver, I've said that to José, and he agrees. And you've been very good to us at this time. And she stopped. It was always like that: Dona Lu would talk her head off and then fall silent in the back seat, quiet.

My father-in-law always had a newspaper under his arm, marking ads for land sales. All of them were either too expensive or too far away. That's what I told him. We've got to do the thing right, I repeated.

Tomorrow, he said, I'm going to talk to a real-estate broker. We'd had lunch and were a bit logy, plopped on the sofa, the entire family, with the television on. I had taken Sulamita home, and we spent the rest of the afternoon watching all that Sunday crap. I fell asleep there, my head leaning on the shoulder of Regina, who was sleeping.

I woke up at seven and Sulamita had gone to the morgue. It was her day to be on duty.

I said goodbye to everyone, I'm going to catch some sleep, I said. Tomorrow I start work early.

Auhnsjfgfl, grunted Regina when I kissed her. How was I supposed to understand that growl?

15

Sunday night. Moacir bellowed. Eliana bellowed, and the children bellowed.

I stood in the hallway, wondering whether or not I should interfere.

Eliana said: She exasperates me. I don't have to put up with that crazy Indian woman, who almost burned my house down. Moacir: Don't change the subject; I wanna know who gave you that piece of meat. And those gizzards.

More shouts. Meats and butcher shops were mentioned. Alceu. Something broke. Glass. And more shouts.

I scratched my head, lit a cigarette. The devil was on the loose. Things are bad today, said a neighbor when he saw me getting out of the car, a retired guy who was all the time poking his nose in where it didn't belong. They've been yelling like that all afternoon, he said.

The name-calling went on and on. Tramp. Drunkard. Bastard. Whore. Limp-dick. It was only when I heard the word "trafficker" that I decided to knock on the door.

Moacir opened the door.

What's happening here? I asked. The neighbors are stirred up.

Moacir came out and closed the door. Eliana continued hurling insults. That woman, he said. Have you heard the rumors? About her and Alceu? You know who Alceu is, the butcher? A kinda cross-eyed guy?

No, I said.

I've had it, he said. The woman's driving me crazy.

I did what I could to calm Moacir, took him for a beer at the corner bar, but to make matters worse, Alceu, the butcher, had the same idea.

See how he looks at me? Then he says he's not looking, he's cross-eyed. Look at him looking over here. I feel like putting out both the bastard's eyes.

The guy's cross-eyed, I said. He's looking at the door, not at us.

He is?

I know those cross-eyed types, I said. You need to calm down. Eliana is an honest woman.

You think so?

Without any doubt.

What about that Alceu guy?

He sells meat, I said. That's all. Cross-eyed.

You think so?

Of course. Eliana loves you, I replied. That's what I'm saying.

We returned home. Moacir seemed to be under control. He said that Ramirez's agent had run into a problem in Paraguay and still hadn't come to pick up the shipment. Careful, I said, you're already talking like a trafficker.

We laughed. Tomorrow, he said, I'm gonna slip you some dough. I've already sold almost a hundred grams today.

We said goodbye, I went up to my room, and when I was almost asleep Carlão phoned me. Are you awake?

More or less.

I want to talk to you.

I felt a chill in my spine. About what?

Can you come here?

Tomorrow?

No. I need your help. Now.

From the look of things, that Sunday had no intention of ending.

Rita's face was like a handful of raw meat, her mouth swollen, bruises; nothing was in order in that face. Her nose was bleeding, and one tooth had been broken. On the sofa, sobbing, she said she was going to lose her child.

Let's take her to the hospital, I told Carlão.

I hope she dies, my cousin said. That bitch. I left my family for her. Two daughters. I hope the baby dies too, that's what I want to happen to that cow.

Carlão left the room. Rita didn't even look at me, sobbing uncontrollably. I moved toward the phone, planning to call an ambulance, but then Carlão returned with a gun. That was when I realized he knew everything.

We're getting out of here, he said. To the car. Both of you. Now.

Take it easy, Carlão. Let's talk, I said.

Now you want to talk, you son of a bitch? You made some poor woman kill herself in São Paulo, I went there, picked you up out of the gutter, brought you here, offered my home, got you a job, you came here, ate my food and took advantage of her being easy, fucked my wife, got my wife pregnant.

I'm not your wife, Rita said.

Shut up, you whore.

You're not my husband, insisted Rita.

The only reason I don't kill the two of you right here and now is 'cause I don't want to dirty my living room with the blood of a couple of pigs. And 'cause I don't want to just kill, I want to bury too. Move it, both of you.

Before going out to the gas station where Carlão's car was, we went through the garage, and he got a shovel and handed it to Rita. I saw blood running down her legs. Stay calm, I said, everything's going to be all right.

In the car, he asked whether if I was spared I would take care of the wretched being that was going to be born, which wouldn't happen because he would kill me along with Rita. That's as sure as two and two is four, he said, but let's suppose I'm a fool and let you two go free?

As soon as I managed to open my mouth to say I was sorry, that neither Rita nor I meant for it to happen, which was a lie – because we had wanted each other from the first day, seeing her sunbathing in a bikini, I was crazy from the first instant, but it was true that I regretted it, that my wish was never to have gotten near Rita – he started yelling, Shut your trap, you goddamn son of a bitch, shut your mouth, you motherfucker, because I swear if I hear your voice I'll kill you both right here and then set fire to the car.

We drove for over twenty minutes, the car being jolted by the dirt road full of potholes, then turned onto a small trail, in even worse condition, and followed it for another ten minutes.

The night was clear and we could see the terrain around us, the trees, the whole landscape. Carlão parked, turned off the headlights, and as soon as we got out, handed the shovel to Rita, ordering her to dig under an *ipê* tree. Keep digging, he said repeatedly. Deeper. Faster. Harder. And when she fell down, he would kick her, saying that she wasn't even any good for that, for digging her own grave. He handed me the shovel.

When the hole was deep enough, Carlão told us to get inside and keep our backs to him.

We obeyed. Sobbing, Rita squeezed my hand.

Let go of his hand, you bitch, screamed Carlão.

I won't, she said. If I'm going to die, I want to die like this.

I tried to pull my hand away, but Rita clutched it tightly.

I closed my eyes, awaiting the worst. And then we heard footsteps in the woods. I thought it was someone approaching but quickly realized the sound was moving away from us.

I gathered my courage and looked behind me and saw Carlão leaving, the gun in his hand.

Rita sobbed, trembling. Stay calm, I said.

I thought we had sunk as low as we could. But things were going to get a lot worse.

16

Collapse, over, I told myself at the hospital. I was trying to stay calm, so was Sulamita. But Sulamita had one curious characteristic. She was capable of sinking into the mud of her own life, to succumb to her private bog, but when it was somebody else in the swamp, she would rise to the occasion, start up her tractor and go about removing and pushing aside the rubble with great ability.

It was she who took the reins in the situation. It was she who called a taxi and came for us after I phoned the morgue, where she was on duty in the middle of the night, telling her what had happened. We had walked for over two hours before finding an inn where we could ask for help. Rita could barely manage to speak. On the way to the hospital I made up a bunch of lies to tell Sulamita, said I was with Carlão and Rita having a beer at their house when they started fighting, that we went to the inn together and Carlão, who was drunk, lost control and had a fit on the way back. Thanks to me, I said, the worst was averted.

At the hospital, after Rita was attended to, Sulamita insisted that I report Carlão. Is that cousin of yours a psychopath? He almost killed the girl. It's very likely she'll lose the baby.

You always ask me why I don't spend time with my cousin, I replied. Now you know. Carlão is crazy, Rita is crazy, their lives are total confusion, and I don't feel like being part of it.

I had been very clear with Rita before Sulamita came for

us at the inn. I said, If you tell Sulamita anything, if you hurt my fiancée – my exact word, fiancée – I'll rearrange your face myself. Afterward I felt sorry for being so coarse. At that moment Rita had ceased to be a girl with a bombastic smile and looked more like a slender thread, an insignificant little thing, but nevertheless her ability to do me in, to grind me into dust, was still enormous.

Rita was in the hospital for three days, and during that time it was Sulamita who looked after her. She took clothes, magazines, fruit, sat at her side and held her hand, saying, Rest easy, you're not going to lose the baby. Everything's all right. You're going to be okay. We're going to help you. Do you want me to let your mother know? Your father? Your brothers and sisters? Rita didn't have anyone, or at least that's what she said. We're your family, said Sulamita, wracked with pity for Rita. We'll take care of you. She repeated that talk of family endlessly.

Do we need to say those things? I whispered in Sulamita's ear. Rita was sleeping, but I was afraid she was just faking. Of course we do, Sulamita answered. She's your cousin. She's not my cousin, I said, Carlão is my cousin. She *is* your cousin. And she could be lying on my table, said Sulamita. Instead of meeting her here, the most likely thing, considering what happened, was that I would receive her there, in the morgue, that way, you know how. Cold. But she's warm. We have to take care of her. Put your hand on her arm, it's warm, isn't it? And she repeated the question as if wanting assurance that Rita was alive. Touch is the real difference, she said. I mean, on my table the touch is the same, it's skin, it's flesh, but it's cold. It looks human, it is human, but the temperature says something else. Disgusting. That was the word she used. And Rita is warm, she continued; we have to be happy about that. Don't you think she's warm?

We spoke softly. Sulamita believed Rita was sleeping, but I saw in that swollen, purplish mouth a certain intent that I knew well, the beginning of Rita's smile, a pilot-smile, the smile of a hooker not worth a plug nickel.

When Rita was released, Sulamita went to fetch her at the hospital. I was loaded down with work at the Berabas' house, Dona Lu was being taken from one doctor to another, not only in Corumbá but also in Campo Grande, and I always went with her. She feels safe with you, the rancher had told me. Actually, José wasn't holding up under the strain. He couldn't bear seeing his wife being eaten alive by the worms of their son's death. Even the police, who earlier had said they would find the man, or the man's body, now held out no hope. They must be betting on the possibility of Junior having disappeared in the river. And José Beraba couldn't take any more suffering. He couldn't stand to see his wife suffer. He went off to his ranch and left his wife dying with me and Dalva. Every day there was a new health problem, a neck pain, another in the temples, in the neck and temples at the same time, her arms numb, tingling in the legs, tachycardia, vomiting, always some new symptom. And new doctors. If Junior were to appear, even dead, I knew the illness would go away. The same thing happened with my mother. At first the sickness is just a fiction, a kind of blackmail the body uses against the mind, and then, over time, it becomes a true cancer. That was what happened to my mother, right before my eyes. Pancreatic cancer. Metathesis. Dona Lu herself told me that for the last twenty-seven years her life had been to love that son. Everything else was secondary. God forgive me, she said, but after my son was born, even He, the Lord Almighty, took second place. First came my son, then everything else. God. Her husband. The memory of her beloved parents. Even herself. What's to become of

83

me? she asked Dalva in the middle of the night, when the cook came to keep her company during the rancher's travels. Her ailment was not yet a disease but a symptom that would become cancer in the future, called "Where is my son?", "I want my son back," "Return my son to me." That was the problem.

I couldn't think about Rita. What are we going to do with her? Sulamita asked upon her release. Rita's a big girl, I replied, she can take care of herself.

That night, when I got to Sulamita's house, I couldn't believe it. Rita, with that slutty face of hers and those peeling red nails, was sitting at the table, dining with my family. My father-in-law and my mother-in-law. And my sister-in-law.

They received and treated Rita with the utmost affection. The utmost consideration. Rita slept in the same room as Regina and had her bed linen and clothes laundered. She needs to eat, said Sulamita's mother. She would bring Rita soup.

All that was making me crazy.

One day, when the two of us were alone in the living room, I said, Look here, Rita, if that stuff about the child being mine is true, you should know I'm not going to acknowledge anything. Take this dough, get that piece of shit out of your belly or else go fuck yourself. Have the brat somewhere far away from me. You don't have the right to fuck up Carlão's life and then fuck up mine. Your plan of serial fucking up our lives is over. Declare victory, I said.

I said these things to Rita expecting her to slap me and throw the money on the floor, but she didn't react. I almost didn't recognize Rita. And where was that laugh of hers?

She's trying to deceive you, over. It was in those days that I began feeling something odd, as if my internal radio, the one that was born inside me when I worked in telemarketing, when I would spend entire days saying over, listening, it was as if that internal radio was beginning to work, to tell me things, independent of my will. A clandestine radio. An interior voice, something that was mine but at the same time independent, spontaneous, telling me: beware, danger. It said: she thinks you're a fool, that you were born yesterday, over. Danger. Danger, over.

My head felt like a pressure cooker. Everything worried me. Rita, Sulamita, Dona Lu, Moacir, the cocaine, everything.

Let's get out of here, I told Sulamita one Friday, and we went to spend the weekend at a bed and breakfast in the region. Moacir had just given me another wad of money and I didn't even consider economizing. Isn't it very expensive? asked Sulamita when we entered the reception area, a cozy setting with a large blue sofa and armchairs with floral patterns where a few tourists were planning outings. This must be very expensive, Sulamita whispered. I lied and said that Dona Lu was a member and had given us the weekend as a present. Sulamita wouldn't let me spend any more money. If we spend, she said, we don't save, and we can only move if we build our nest egg. And don't spend. Save and spend. And economize. She repeated that all the time like it was a prayer.

But I was spending everything, I couldn't control myself. Serafina had asked me for money to visit her tribe, I paid for the visit. My father-in-law asked for money to repair his roof, I paid for the repair. Don't say anything to Sulamita, he said. And afterward he asked for more money, I didn't really understand for what, and I gave it to him. Later he said he was going to build a room in the rear, for Sulamita and me, and I gave him more money. If my father asks you for money, don't give it to him, warned Sulamita. I suspect, she said, that my father has a second family. She spoke too late: the old man had already gotten a good piece of dough for his lover. If he actually had a lover.

Even today, when I close my eyes, I remember that weekend. We only left the room to hike trails and swim. I spent the morning floating in the lake, feeling the sun on my body, and after lunch we would sleep and make love. Sulamita sometimes left to go horseback riding, but I stayed in the room, thinking that everything was going to be all right, over. Not everything, over. Be careful, over. My premonitions, I thought, were a false alarm. They're real, over. Be careful. They're not real, I repeated. After all, who wouldn't be impressed at seeing so much suffering? Good thing, I thought, that it was Rita who suffered, that it was Carlão who suffered, that it was Dona Lu who suffered, over. Better them than me, I thought. So far everything is fine, I thought. I'm safe in that bedroom with blue curtains, with everything blue like the blue sky outside. Black, over.

When we returned on Sunday night we found Sulamita's mother saddened. Rita went away, she said with a disconsolate expression. She said to give you a hug. I really like that girl, my mother-in-law said, she was so patient with Regina.

Did she leave a letter? I asked.

No, just a hug.

I left there devastated, feeling like crap. How could I have treated the pregnant Rita that way? I didn't know where to look for her, and the absurd idea occurred to me of asking for Carlão's help. I even called my cousin, but I hung up when he answered the phone in a drunken voice. Carlão had been drinking lately. And crying at the door of his ex-wife. That's what I was told.

That night I sat out in front of the workshop, hoping she would appear. Time passed, and in the darkness, as I looked at the deserted street and the line of telephone poles, all that existed was a strange silence that only allowed me to hear my heart throbbing in my head.

It was already getting light when I went to my room. And as soon as I lay down, the shouting began. Fuck them, I thought, burying my head under the pillows.

I didn't get up until I heard the sirens.

I went downstairs just as I was, in shorts, without a shirt. Moacir had given Eliana a beating; it must be the thing in Corumbá to beat your wife. That was how couples got along, by beatings. Drawing blood.

Two policemen were talking, leaning against the patrol car, while two other cops, inside the house, were trying to defuse the situation.

I stood there, tense, disguising my feelings with small talk, thinking only about the drugs.

He's a good guy, I said.

There's women who deserve being slapped around, agreed one of the cops.

Some of 'em even like it, said the other.

We laughed, and I thought the matter would end there.

But then one of the cops inside the house came out and asked for handcuffs.

We found ten kilos of powder here with the perp, he said.

Ten kilos. Almost ten kilos.

What world does a dead man belong to? T'other world.
What world does money belong to? This world.

CHARLES DICKENS
Our Mutual Friend

Part II

THE THIEF

Part II

17

How much you got? asked Ramirez.

We were back on the veranda of his factory, in Puerto Suárez. The sewers in that region are exposed, and the stench of excrement filled the air. I felt dizzy, I had gotten lost on the way, right, left, right, left again, trying to remember the route taken on my first visit, but I got mixed up, I took chances more than once and got confused, I had to return to downtown and phone Juan, write down the directions, and now there I was, feeling awkward, sweating, it's going to end up in shit, over.

Juan listened to our conversation while he taught two women how to work the press. A third woman, younger and fatter, used an electric clipper to cut Ramirez's hair very short so that his shock of black hair stood up like the bristles of a broom.

Be clear, insisted Ramirez. I hate it when anybody starts with "I think." I wanna know exactly how much you've got to give me.

I didn't have anything, I'd spent it all. Moacir, when I visited him in prison the day before, had said the same thing, nothing, he'd spent everything, paying creditors, nothing, nothing was left, he'd said. Installments on the refrigerator, the television, the washing machine; Moacir's house looked like the showroom of an appliance store. All because of that bitch, he had said. I do everything to please the woman and it doesn't do any good, she's cuckolding me, I found a note from the butcher setting up a meeting with her behind the butcher shop. "I love you too" was in the note, Moacir had said, shaken.

I had gone to see him to talk about our problem, to ask Moacir to keep his mouth shut, to not get me involved in anything, and also to see what we could do about Ramirez, but Moacir was only concerned with Eliana, he'd gone crazy over the fact of his wife being in love with the butcher. If Alceu wrote "I love you too," he said, emphasizing the word *too*, it's because Eliana's been telling him "I love you." Don't you think?

I tried to bring him back to reality. How are we going to get you out of here? I asked more than once. I'd rather be a prisoner than see Eliana with Alceu, he replied. How can I look people in the eye? My neighbors? What are they gonna say? And my kids?

Fuck Eliana, I told Moacir. Kick the bitch out. On top of everything else she's ugly as sin.

Ugly? Eliana? Moacir didn't like hearing that, he was the only one who could bad-mouth his obese dwarf. Don't offend Eliana, he answered. Eliana is my life, and it's not even her fault. I know my wife, she wouldn't fall for a cross-eye like Alceu, who's all the time hauling goat on his back. The butcher shop is the thing. She's in love with the butcher shop. I keep wondering, is the butcher shop really his?

Now, in front of Ramirez, I made an effort to understand what was being said, our conversation wasn't fluent, I was nervous and several times my Spanish tripped over my ideas, I got confused, and to make matters worse, the noise of the electric clippers also got in the way. What? I repeated, uncertain, what're you saying?

Is Porco deaf? Ramirez said, exasperated, and Juan was forced to put the press aside and use his Portunhol to translate the trafficker's words.

It's very simple, Ramirez said, Moacir told me your wife works for the police, isn't that right? Talk to your wife, tell her to give back the confiscated drugs. I stumbled over that part, it never entered my head to put Sulamita in the middle of things. The first thing that occurred to me was that I was an idiot; how could I ever have relied on Moacir? We think the devil comes in the back door, that he comes with your enemies, but the truth is that we ourselves open the door to him the moment we trust someone. Goddamn Indian. Blabbermouth. What's the name of your wife? asked Ramirez. Ex-wife, I replied. Ex, I repeated, I'm separated, actually we weren't married, just lovers. She worked in the precinct as an administrative assistant, I explained, but now she's at the morgue.

Ah, Porco, that's gotta be why you were caught, concluded Ramirez. I'm gonna tell you something: you shouldn't have separated. No woman likes a kick in the ass. She ratted you out. That's what happened.

I didn't kick anybody in the ass, I said, and I wasn't caught. Moacir was arrested, not me.

I don't give a shit what happened, Ramirez said. You're costing me money.

Ramirez spoke without looking at me, gazing only at the mirror in his hands. The front part of his hair was already looking like a perfect brush, but the back part hadn't been trimmed yet and appeared more like a vulture's wing.

Just look at the situation you're putting me in, Porco. You showed up here, took ten kilos on consignment.

Five, I said. Ten, he insisted, it was part of our agreement to deliver the other five in Corumbá. And that didn't happen. Twice my runner tried to pick up the drugs, which were gonna be taken to Araraquara, and Moacir wasn't there. And now you tell me the shipment got seized. And

93

that you don't have no way to pay. When your girlfriend blew the whistle on us – Hold on, I interrupted, she didn't blow the whistle on anybody. I told him about the argument between Moacir and his wife. It was because of the fight that the police showed up, I insisted, there wasn't any squealing. Of course there was. It was your girlfriend.

Now the hair-clipping machine seemed to be inside my head, cutting into my thoughts. I was sweating, soaking my work shirt. I'm going to have to make a stop at home before returning to the Barabas', I thought.

Let's continue the conversation, he said. First: Moacir has to keep his trap shut, 'cause if he talks, I fear for his life. Guys who talk a lot, I hear, die hung in their cells. A shame, but it happens. Second: you two owe me fifty thousand dollars. Thirty for the product and twenty for the loss. And third: I'll give you a month, not a day longer, to come up with the money. I'm doing you a favor. I like Moacir. Fourth: if you don't pay, be very clear about it, I'll go to your home and kill you. You worthless Porco, I'll kill your girlfriend, her relatives, I'll kill Moacir's family and feel avenged. Now get outta here so I can cut my hair in peace.

On the road back, I felt totally discouraged: you're fucked, over. Where am I going to find fifty thousand dollars? I had an enormous desire to be with Rita, on a boat, listening to the sound of the water. Where must Rita be?

On the radio they said that N.K., an Englishwoman, cashier at a supermarket, had just won two million pounds in the lottery, which is almost eight million in our currency. A pity, I thought, that it happened to N.K. and not to me. Really bad things, I thought – and really good things – only happen to others. Only others have their heads cut off by the blades of a helicopter. Only others lose almost everything in the stock market. On the other hand, only others make a killing in the stock market. Or the lottery. Only others. Life is others, I thought. Others. We, the rest, remain here, seeing and hearing about their lives in celebrity magazines and the news on TV.

My only solution, I thought as I passed a truck that was falling apart, my only solution is Dona Lu. What if I had a talk with her? What if I told her the truth? Dona Lu was always saying she liked me. She likes you to drive her car, over. To open and close doors. To say thank you, yes ma'am. Certainly. If I were Junior, I thought, she'd pay. You're not Junior, over. Junior is the others, over. Them. The ones who have helicopters. The drugs, though, were Junior's, I thought to myself. I mean, not specifically those drugs, but the ones before, the ones that had already been sold. In a way, Junior was involved in my imbroglio. Thinking about it, if not for Junior I wouldn't be in that mess.

At home, when I changed clothes, already late for work, I saw I didn't have any money. I climbed into the crawl space to get the last few bills Moacir had given me before his arrest. And there I saw Junior's backpack.

I got it, dumped the contents on my bed: credit cards, key ring, ID card, driver's license. I looked at the photos in the documents. Good-looking guy, Junior. Handsome. I put on the sunglasses and went to look at myself in the mirror. Only they are born rich. The Juniors. Only they crash in their private planes.

I turned on the cell phone. *You have new messages* appeared on the screen. Enter your code, said the recording. I tried the day and year of Junior's birth. Nothing. The messages were released when I typed part of his ID number. Son, said Dona Lu, what time are you arriving? Your father wants to have dinner earlier, he's traveling tomorrow. Call me. I love you, my dear. Another message, from Daniela, his girlfriend:

Hi, love. Gil invited us to his house today. Ricky and Laura are going too. Gabi's here also. When you get in, call me at home.

The other messages were from Dona Lu, and it was obvious they'd been left after the accident. Actually, they were nothing but sobs, moans, a throbbing pain that penetrated the soul like a sharp object. If I had to define the moment when the idea of blackmailing Dona Lu first entered my head, I'd say it was then, in bed, listening to those recordings. My sensation was that something came to the surface at that moment, a part of me submerged in the depths of my swamp, the evil, over. And what if you blackmail the family, over? What if you say you know where the body is? And ask for money in exchange for the body? Over.

I liked Dona Lu a lot, but that didn't keep me from having that horrible idea. That, I thought, is nothing but pure iniquity, and I'm a good person. If I'm not good, I thought, at least I'm not the worst. I'm a regular type. Almost good. I'm neutral, to tell the truth. I always sin. Yes, I did push that telemarketer into the abyss. With a slap. Yes, I had an affair with my cousin's wife. I've lied a lot in my life. But I don't do certain things. I don't kill. I don't steal. I'm incapable of taking advantage of a mother's pain. Or blackmailing a mother who's suffering. Money, over. From the cadaver of her own son. Opportunity, over. A mother you know and who's called Dona Lu. Fifty thousand dollars, over. If that vileness was inside me, trying to break out, I would put an end to it.

You're being stupid, over. That's what my internal radio, which it was no longer possible to turn off, was saying. I would think and my private interlocutor, over, would counter, always trying to show me I was wrong, that goodness, over, like God, was a fantasy, that man is born bad and gets worse with time, and that I should forge ahead with my diabolical plan.

I was still in a state of confusion. I had changed clothes and was soaked again, ready to get back to work, but without the heart to face the heat outside. I'm going to phone the Berabas, I thought, and say I don't feel very good, and at just that moment Dalva called me on my cell phone.

Where are you? she said. Distressed, she asked me to go to the hospital. It was urgent.

I put everything back in the crawl space and dashed out.

18

Horrible, horrible, said Dalva when I got to the hospital. That girl, Junior's girlfriend, came to the house this morning. Dona Lu had started the day well; I even managed to get her to drink a little milk. We went for a stroll in the garden, she took some sun on the veranda, she was really in good shape, we talked, she asked if you were going to get there soon, said she'd like to go to church. I thought, It's going to be a better day, but then Daniela arrived. You know how Dani is, I've never seen anyone so spoiled, such a pampered girl, she arrived fresh from the beauty salon, her toenails and finger-nails painted with the greatest care, you could even smell the polish, you know? Fresh nail polish? And she started saying how she was suffering, depressed, how she couldn't stand it anymore, and me just looking at those red nails. The girl goes for a manicure and then suffers? All manicured? That's what I don't understand. Suffering doesn't have red fingernails. Look at Dona Lu. The woman doesn't even brush her teeth if I don't put the paste on the toothbrush, she can't even do that herself. Combing her hair. I'm the one who dresses Dona Lu. And the other woman going to the manicurist. Right away the two of them were crying, hugging, I called the girl aside and said, Listen, Dani, it'd be better for you to leave, Dona Lu is very weak, she can't handle so much emotion. But Dani acted like she didn't hear, hugged me, cried and stood there, sobbing, complaining about life like she was a widow. When she left, Dona Lu had to lie down, you know, the poor thing is so thin, so frail that she can't stay on her feet. When I went to take her soup at lunchtime, I found her fallen beside the empty boxes of medicine she had swallowed. Horrible.

I was devastated, not only because of Dona Lu but for having spent the morning thinking about some way of deceiving that woman who had just attempted suicide. And she liked me. Trusted me. How could I do anything bad to Dona Lu?

Dalva left to buy fruit and José went home to take a bath. I won't be long, he said. I was by myself in the waiting room, observing the movement of the nurses.

It was more or less four in the morning when I heard a rustling; Dona Lu was as silent as an old cat. I went into the room and found her awake. I asked if she needed anything. I explained that José and Dalva must already be back and that I wouldn't leave, she could rest easy. She smiled in a helpless way. I took her hand and said I understood perfectly what they were going through. And I began telling the story of my father, in a way I'd never done. For years, it was as if I were ashamed of what had happened with my father. How can a person wake up, have breakfast, kiss his wife and son, leave for work saying See you later, and never return? To me it always seemed I was the problem, not my father. My mother. She was the problem. The two of us, together and wrapped up in each other, constituted a heavy burden for my father. And afterward, I must say, I had a hard time understanding a finish like that. That's not how people end, I thought. It was a system failure. Somebody's mistake. That's what I thought, but that day I told the story in different terms. Maybe because it seemed to me, at least there in the hospital, that Dona Lu and I belonged to the same club of those who don't know what happened to members of their family. The club of the last to know. I surprised myself with my courage that day. It takes a certain amount of impudence to talk about abandonment, even when no one is to blame. I spoke without embarrassment, told how my father left the house and evaporated like ether, how he didn't even show up at the shoe store where he was manager. We're terrified, the saleswomen told my mother. We don't know what to do with the orders. The payments. Where are the records? He left with just the clothes on his back, we repeated, as if that somehow proved we weren't involved in the disappearance. And at night, in bed, my mother sobbed, hugging me, and said that something terrible had happened to daddy, something very awful, she said, which filled me with fear. I imagined something so frightening that it couldn't even be visualized, it wasn't like a fire, a shooting, it was worse, it was evil in its essence, its definitive form, as implacable as a fall into the abyss. If he were alive, she would say, he'd phone me. But the fact is that my father never called. We never found out whether he died, whether he was murdered, whether he was run over and buried as an indigent or ran away with another woman.

I also spoke of the regular visits to hospitals and police stations, the false leads, the wild goose chases, our unceasing hope that only ended the day my mother died. When I buried my mother, I buried my father too. In the same grave. It was necessary to bury my father, I said. That was very important. The funeral. Without burial, at least a symbolic one, I wouldn't have been able to go on.

Dona Lu's eyes were closed, she seemed not to hear. I went on talking for a time, until I noticed the tears running down her face and falling onto the pillow.

The nurse came in to apply an injection and asked Dona Lu if she preferred that I leave. She didn't answer but grasped my hand, not strongly, but she grasped it. I waited for her to take the medication and left when I saw she was asleep.

Later, Daniela came to visit, bringing flowers and chocolate. She's sleeping, I said. Daniela sat beside me in her tight pants, hair down to her waist. She radiated wealth, Daniela. Wealth came out of her pores and shone before us like purpurin.

I've lost hope, she said.

About what?

Junior is dead. We're not going to find him.

And why did you come here?

What?

Why do you go on messing up Dona Lu's life?

I spoke without thinking, but once I had spoken, I forged ahead, asked why she continued visiting Dona Lu, tormenting Dona Lu, why she didn't get on with her own life, find another boyfriend, travel to Europe. It'll be better for everyone, I said. Leave Dona Lu be.

Daniela started to cry.

But I lost patience.

I'm going to get some coffee, I said. If you want to leave, wait for the nurse or someone from the family.

While I drank an espresso I thought about the large number of dying people there. Many would never return home. It was just a matter of time. From there, they would go straight to the cemetery. If I could at least find a body, over, I could go forward with my plan.

I'm not going to do anything of the sort, I thought. Yes, you are, over. Nothing of the sort. No way. Never. Not to Dona Lu. I don't do such things. All my life I felt I was made of ordinary stuff, the type who's abandoned by his father, but that's a lot different from being bad. I'm not perverse. A rapist, an alcoholic. A psychopath. Kidnapper. Thief. I lack the courage to do certain things. To kidnap. There's a limit to everything. Rape. In dealing with goodness, if I'm not neutral, at least I'm unimportant. Which is great, morally speaking. Being a zero is better than being negative. Minus five, minus ten. On the scale of evil. Especially in today's world. Evil everywhere. I shouldn't count at a time like this. I must be part of the group that, if there were actually a Day of Judgment, doesn't deserve either heaven or hell. I'll be left right here on Earth. The kind that's neither fish nor fowl.

But what about Sulamita? Sulamita could get a cadaver for me, over. It doesn't matter how much I might tell myself that I'm incapable of doing certain things, my clandestine radio went on broadcasting, putting horrible ideas in my head. You think there's a big distance between thinking and acting. You tell yourself that thinking isn't doing, you say: I'm just thinking scabrous things, which doesn't mean I'm going to do scabrous things. And that's how plans are born. It's merely a mental exercise, you say. You set everything up and at H-hour pull back. You elaborate a hideous plan that basically consists of taking advantage of the suffering of people in mourning. The details are macabre: you call Dona Lu, over, and say you know where her son's body is. You tell a believable story about a fisherman who found a body in the waters of the Paraguay. You tell Dona Lu, If you want your son back, you'll have to pay. $200,000.

With the money I would pay off my debt and straighten out my life. The more I moved ahead with my macabre plan, the more disgusted I felt. And attracted. How could I think of something as absurd as that?

At the end of the afternoon, when I parked my car in front of Moacir's bicycle shop, Serafina came out to speak to me. She had just returned from visiting her tribe and was worried about her son. At least that's what I imagined she was saying as I climbed the stairs that led to my room. She was so nervous she only managed to speak Guató. Stay calm, Serafina, everything's going to be taken care of, I said, dying to be alone for a while.

It was only when I finally got rid of the Indian woman that I noticed the presence of Sulamita, sitting on my bed.

Hi, she said, showing me Junior's backpack.

Can you explain to me what this is?

19

It was Sulamita's day off and she had decided to wait for me at my place. She had arrived around three and had straightened up the room. I organized your drawers, she said, changed the sheets, cleaned the bathroom, and when I was lying on the bed watching television, after taking a bath, I heard a phone ring. And it wasn't mine. I noticed that the sound was coming from the ceiling. I got a chair, opened the crawl space, and in the area under the roof found the backpack with the telephone and documents of the pilot who disappeared.

From the tin roof came waves of hot air that drained my strength. I took off my shirt and lay down beside Sulamita.

Next time turn the phone off before hiding it, over. If she wanted the truth, it was very easy, I thought, all I had to do was open my mouth, over. The words gushed forth without difficulty or censorship. I told her everything that had happened, spoke of the fishing trip on the Paraguay River, the explosion in the sky, the plane crashing and how the man died before my very eyes. I spoke of my attempt to save him. Know why you found the safety belt undone and the doors open? I asked. Because I tried to save him. I repeated that information with a degree of pride, I wanted Sulamita to understand that before anything else I had tried to help the pilot, but she kept interrupting me. Why didn't you call the police? Why are you working for his family? You're lying, she said. What about this backpack? And this cell phone? She didn't even wait for an answer. Stop, I said, stop and listen.

Don't touch me, she said.

My mistake, I said, was undoing the safety belt, and if I'm to be judged, let it be for that, and for leaving the plane's doors open. As for the cell phone and the backpack, what could he do with them? I asked. He was dead, I said. I thought they wouldn't be missed, either by him or the family.

You were in that plane, she stated, you saw that young man.

I recounted everything again, explained that the pilot had probably been swept away by the current and devoured by piranhas. That's my theory, I said.

Outside, the children were jumping rope, and for a moment the only sound was the lashing against the pavement, synchronized with the beating of my heart. Without heeding the consequences, I told the rest of the story, said I'd found a kilo of powder inside the plane, had sold the drug, which was why I hadn't reported the accident to the police. I spoke of my deal with Ramirez, said that Moacir was my partner, and went on talking until coming to the conversation I'd had with the Bolivian that morning. As I advanced, Sulamita withdrew, prostrate, as if my words were some kind of paralyzing gas. At the end she was sitting on my bed, her head in her hands, staring at the floor, saying that it wasn't possible. It's not possible, she repeated.

I also told of my job and how I ended up at the Berabas' house. I said something about vultures and rotting flesh. Deep down, I said, I must miss seeing my mother cry, maybe this job is so I can suffer with Dona Lu the same way I suffered with my mother, maybe the vicarious pain is a form of vicarious pleasure, I said, but didn't use those words, I wasn't clear. I spoke of my mother and my father, of how

105

much I missed them both, mixed everything with Dona Lu and ended with promises. Nothing's going to change, I said, we're going to go ahead with our plans, deep down I didn't do anything wrong, I'm making the greatest effort possible, I said, you have to trust me.

I felt an enormous sense of peace after dumping my steaming sin on Sulamita. It was as if the burden was now hers as well, mine and hers, as much ours as the idea of marriage that she had shoved down my throat, I thought. I sat on the bed, tried to hug her, but she moved away. I ought to leave here and go straight to the precinct, said Sulamita.

We remained silent for a time, then she asked me, how could you go behind my back? It has nothing to do with you, I replied, and she continued to inquire: What's going to happen now? What's going to happen to you? To me?

If you help me, I said, we can find a way out of this.

How? She wanted to know. You think you're up to fooling the police, deceiving Junior's family, getting around the traffickers, outwitting everybody? How are you going to get fifty thousand dollars to pay Ramirez?

I asked if there was any way of getting the powder back. What are you talking about? she screamed. Do you think I can just waltz into the station, grab the drugs and say, "Joel, this belongs to my boyfriend?" Good God, you don't have a clue about anything. You're crazy.

Maybe, I said, if you explained to your friends at the station —, over, but I didn't have the heart to continue. At that moment Sulamita threw herself face down on the bed, sobbing, saying I had no right to do that to her life, to her family. How do you find the courage to ruin everything like that? To destroy my dreams? I haven't destroyed anything, I said, everything I did was for the two of us. Stop that nonsense, she said, you're an egotist.

106

All of it was making me sick: the heat, Sulamita's crying, and there outside, the knife-sharpener working at his emery wheel. I thought it wouldn't be a bad idea to sharpen my knives, just to get away from there.

At the exact moment I had this thought, Sulamita got up, grabbed her things, and left. She slammed the door without even bothering to say goodbye.

20

I took a cold shower, and it left me more agitated than before. I didn't get any sleep all night. It was very hot, and I tossed and turned in bed, thinking about what to do. What if Sulamita turned me in? What if Ramirez killed me? The hottest day of the year, the radio said. It said: sixteen trampled to death at a religious event. It said: Taliban stronghold invaded. It said: Iran enriches uranium to twenty percent.

So far, so good, I told myself. I'm not religious, I'm not an insurgent, and I don't live in Iran. And it's still possible to run away, to return to São Paulo, over. Go back to telemarketing. Sell novelties that nobody wants to buy.

I felt a weird sensation that alternated between deep despair and an artificial calm. As soon as I relaxed I became nervous again, I would go out into the street, smoke a cigarette, walk to the corner, trying to get rid of that affliction, thinking that the most that could happen to me was to be killed by Ramirez, go to prison, or return to São Paulo. The "anti-city." That was how I thought of São Paulo. The counter-city that had turned me into an anti-I. Capable of slapping female employees. Still, it was one option. Besides, even if they hunted me down and arrested me, there was a limit to misfortune. They – Ramirez and the police – couldn't arrest me twice or kill me twice, I told myself, so that's all, prison or death, as if prison and death were just meaningless words. That's how I calmed myself. And suddenly it was as if I had woken up from a state of confusion and understood exactly what it meant to go to prison and to die. Or to return to São Paulo.

Saturday morning I went to the supermarket with Serafina, bought ham, bread, crackers, and cigarettes, and then we left for the penitentiary to visit Moacir.

He was even more dejected than at our first meeting and very worried about the children. He'd made his mother promise she'd take care of the kids. Don't let Eliana hit them, he said, Eliana is very high-strung. Serafina wanted to know what was going on and asked a lot of questions. Mother, he answered, it doesn't do any good to explain. All you've gotta do is take care of the children, that's all.

At the end, he asked his mother to give us a few moments and told me it had been Eliana who blew the whistle on him. How do you know? I asked. She told me so herself, she was here yesterday. Does she know about me? I asked. No, he replied, of course not. She saw the packages of drugs in my workshop and when we were fighting, when the cops arrived, she ratted me out. That's what happened.

Then his eyes turned red, he made an effort not to cry as he told me that Eliana had stated plainly that she had turned him in because she hated him. She said she's disgusted by me, he continued, that I'm like a dirty pig in the middle of those bikes. Since when is grease dirty?

I didn't know what to say. Maybe it's a lie, I ventured. It's grease, he said. I tried to calm him, I said I'd talk with Sulamita, see about finding a lawyer, and he told me it wasn't necessary, that he had already taken care of everything. How? I asked. A friend of mine, you don't know him. I urged him not to involve me. Are you crazy? he said. Who's gonna take care of my kids? Or my mother? I'm counting on you, he said.

I was disconcerted by his answer. It wasn't part of my plans to take care of Moacir's family, and from the way things were put, the price of my freedom would be something like marrying Eliana. Taking on her children.

Don't let them lack for anything, he said.

Of course not, I agreed. Never.

I left with Serafina still confused, asking more questions.

When we arrived, we found Eliana returning from the outdoor market with the little Indians, each one with a turnover in his hand. I asked if she needed anything and she told me the only thing she wanted was to be rid of Serafina. I can't put up with that old woman in my house any longer, she said.

I took Serafina to have lunch nearby, but neither of us managed to eat a bite.

Later, I called Sulamita. What's going on? asked my father-in-law at the other end of the line. She's acting strange. Quiet. Come over here so we can talk, the old man continued, maybe I can help you two. I give good advice. I'm your friend. By the way, I need a favor from you. Father to son. An advance, he said, as if I were his boss. The chance to buy my neighbor's VW has come up. Can't do it right now, I said. And tell Sulamita I called, over.

I spent the rest of the day in my room, with Serafina beside me, silently braiding straw, and at certain moments her presence was even comforting. From time to time, when I closed my eyes, my plan, over, slowly formed like a gigantic wave that started through a crack in my tectonic plates in the deepest and darkest part of my ocean and came rushing forward, gaining force and volume. The argument for me to go ahead was also powerful: if I had been rich when my father disappeared, and if at the time someone had phoned to propose a trade, my money for my father's body, I wouldn't have hesitated for a second. I'd have paid. My plan, per se, wouldn't do any harm to Dona Lu. She had money to burn. In a way, I'd even be doing the family a favor, since it's by burying our dead that they die once and for all and leave us in peace. The problem, over, was the cadaver. Where to find a cadaver?

Sunday was worse than Saturday. Sulamita didn't answer my calls. I felt numb, torpid, and heavy because of the heat.

Serafina brought me a cold fish broth. While I ate it, in bed, the Indian woman taught me, for the first time, an expression in Guató, *infani*, whose meaning, she explained, was "it's awful."

I only got out of bed when, around three o'clock, Dalva phoned, asking if I could pick up José at the airport.

On the way back, the rancher told me how worried he was about Dona Lu's health. I know, he said, I know deep down that Junior is dead, but she won't believe it until she sees our son's body. The word "body" infused me with courage. Act quickly, over.

When I returned home, the Indian kids were in my bedroom, playing hide-and-seek. I threw everyone out and lay down, my head roiling with ideas.

And then, at seven o'clock, I heard a sound on the stairs.

I ran to open the door and saw Sulamita coming toward me.

As I embraced her, I noticed from the sour smell of her clothes and hair that she had come from the morgue.

She took my hand and said she needed to show me something. It's very important.

Infani, I thought, as we headed out to my car.

21

Sulamita pulled back the sheet, uncovering the naked body of Moacir on the morgue table.

I stepped back in sudden panic, unable to take my eyes off the coarsely sewn cut that began at the pubis and ended high in the chest. That was what I was afraid of, over. The legs had also been cut open and stitched. It's a common procedure in the autopsy of people who suffer violent deaths, Sulamita explained.

I could barely keep my balance, I was sweating, nauseated at the putrid smell mixed with bleach. It's the end, I thought, supporting myself against the wall.

Eliana doesn't know yet, she said. And while she told me that Moacir had been found in his cell, tied to a sheet attached to the bars on the window, a single idea came into my head: I was next.

It was this morning, Sulamita continued, when the prisoners were sunning themselves in the courtyard.

They're going to kill me, I said. They're sending me a message.

You think, she answered, that didn't occur to me when I saw Moacir on the table? That I didn't think about you and everything you told me the day before yesterday? I wasn't even supposed to be at the autopsy. I was just leaving my shift. I asked Rosana, the coroner who works here, to let me follow the procedure. I did more than that; I called Joel and asked to read the inquest.

I asked Sulamita if a suicide couldn't be faked. Maybe, I said, maybe someone tied a sheet to those bars and forced Moacir to hang himself.

Know what we do when a cadaver arrives here? Sulamita said. We sit down beside it and have a chat. A corpse tells all. We turn it inside out, rip it from head to toe, take out the viscera, scalp it, pull out the brain. Look, she said, indicating a deep, irregular groove in Moacir's neck. This mark is the sign of hanging. If it were a crime, it would be around the entire neck, not just in front. And there would be signs of a struggle. Look here, she said, pointing to the shoulder region, there are no scratches or contusions.

I need protection, I insisted. They killed Moacir, whatever you may have seen in the autopsy. The Bolivians told me they were going to kill him.

I told her in detail about my conversation with Ramirez, said that I'd be the next one and that if I didn't pay the debt I'd be found floating in the river or hanged like Moacir. I need police protection, I said. I repeated it several times, begging her to believe me, and the more Sulamita asked me to stay calm, the more nervous I became. I said: You're like those detectives in bad crime movies that get in the way of the investigation and let innocent people die.

Who's innocent? You? she asked. I didn't like the way she said it.

I was shaking uncontrollably. You don't understand, I said. I need protection.

You're the one who doesn't understand, she interrupted. Stop talking nonsense. It was a suicide, and it isn't the police or the Bolivians saying it. It's me. Yours truly. And what's this idiotic talk about protection? Do you by some chance want to go to the precinct and confess you're the owner of the cocaine found at Moacir's? Is that your plan? If it is, go right

113

ahead. Because those guys only provide protection – and it's crappy protection that's not going to solve anything if somebody really wants to kill you – if you go there and do what Moacir never did at any time. Open his mouth. Moacir was very decent. He protected you.

The idea of turning myself in didn't strike me as totally bad. But if they had killed Moacir inside the penitentiary, why wouldn't they kill me too?

Sulamita took me outside. Go to the car, she said. She returned minutes later with a Coca-Cola. You've got to understand one thing, she said. I really did check. I went to the penitentiary after the autopsy. I spoke to Joel. I spoke with Alfredo, the jailer who found Moacir in the morning. He told me that when he went into the cell, Moacir still had an erection, he had just ejaculated. Yes, it was suicide, she said. All the elements point to suicide.

We stood there, with me trembling and drinking Coca-Cola, while I thought about whether there was some way for me to escape.

The only way out was my plan. Project Cadaver, over.

22

The day was rainy, but even so, people kept on arriving. Some merely looked at the deceased and left. Others weren't satisfied with that little and wanted details about the suicide. They came not because they had known or liked the bicycle repairman but because it wasn't often that someone killed themselves in those parts. I thought, observing the amusement of the intruders, people here don't kill themselves, they just die. From a shot to the chest. That's how they die. They fall from scaffolding. They're run over. Or they simply rot. If I had to kill myself, said one old woman, it would never be with a rope. Even dogs kill each other, another said.

The coffin sat between the stove and the sofa. Serafina, who had spent the night keeping vigil over the body, was now dozing, leaning over the corpse.

Sitting beside Alceu, Eliana buzzed constantly like some happy bee. Whispering in Alceu's ear the entire time, she paid no attention to anyone but the butcher, not even looking at her husband's corpse.

Stop staring at her, said Sulamita, you don't have anything to do with it.

She can't act that way, I said. Not in front of everybody.

You're not one of the family.

I'm paying for the burial, I insisted, the coffin, the flowers, the tomb. She could at least show respect for the deceased.

I must have been talking too loud. Now Eliana and Alceu were looking at me. Let's go get some coffee, Sulamita said.

I had been drinking coffee all night. I was swimming in coffee, nervous, irritated. And had a headache.

We left and I felt the light rain cool my body.

Those guys over by the lamp post, I told Sulamita. You see them?

What about them?

I've never seen them before in this neighborhood.

You're making me nervous, she replied.

I left Sulamita talking to herself, went back into Moacir's house, woke up Serafina and took her to the window. I know them, she said, they live in the neighborhood.

When I went back outside, Sulamita said I needed to calm down.

Why don't you believe me? I asked.

For God's sake, he killed himself. How many times do I have to tell you that he wasn't murdered, he killed himself. Moacir was in a bind and he killed himself. That's what happened.

But I'm in danger, I insisted. They want to kill me. And if I die, if I turn up dead, don't say I didn't warn you.

At ten o'clock we got in the car, following the undertaker in the black hearse carrying Moacir's body. At that exact moment, a deluge burst over the city.

At the cemetery, only Eliana and Alceu plus the children had umbrellas. The others, few in number, watched in the falling rain as the gravedigger lowered the body into what seemed like a muddy reservoir.

After the burial, I saw Eliana leaving hurriedly with the children, at Alceu's side. Serafina followed her, but I saw Eliana say something to her in a stern manner.

I approached and asked if there was a problem.

There's no room for her in the car, said Eliana.

She turned her back and walked away, the widow. The merry widow incarnate.

Before parking in front of the bike shop, I asked Serafina to look around. Look carefully, I said, make sure there's no stranger nearby, over. Behind the car. Look there. The other side of the street. On the corner. It wouldn't be a bad idea to get a gun, I thought, as I quickly got out of the van.

I called Dalva to say I wouldn't return to work, and spent the rest of the day in bed. A lot of things were still confused in my head. Maybe I should quit my job with the Berabas. So as not to arouse suspicions later on, at H-hour. The problem is that from the outside, over, the view is different. The particulars get lost. Besides which, an abrupt departure could arouse suspicions. Maybe later on, some detective in the Pantanal, a Joel in boots and hat, would turn up saying "funny that the Berabas' driver quit at that moment rather than some other." But it's also true that the opposite could occur and I would be suspect not for leaving but for staying. For being Sulamita's boyfriend. Sulamita, of all people, who's in charge of the morgue. So, I told myself, I have to do some figuring before I act. Weigh up the pros and cons. But the truth is, there's something that can't be measured.

Whenever an airliner crashes I think about the people who get to the airport early and have the chance to move up their trip. Wouldn't they be trading a sure, safe flight for the one that's going to plunge into the ocean and kill 198 passengers? The worst airline crash ever, the experts will say. Things could also have happened the other way around. And precisely because he didn't move up his flight, the guy dies. Because the plane marked with an X was that one and

117

not this one. And there are even worse variations. Maybe it's his presence that determines the crash. Maybe our fate is written in our DNA. Maybe God is just settling accounts with you and all the others are going to die as supporting players on whatever flight you take.

That's what I mean. Logic, intelligence, strategy, and plans all exist, but there's also the mystery of life. The truth is that we can only go so far. Beyond that, it's luck. And luck is luck. That's what I was thinking in the shower when there was a knock at the door.

I wrapped a towel around me, left the bathroom, and remained quiet for several moments, with the lights out. It's me, said Sulamita. Open the door.

On the way back from the cemetery, two hours earlier, I had dropped her off at home and felt something in the air, something unspoken, as if Sulamita found odd the fact that I didn't even ask if she wanted to go to my place. Ever since the day she discovered the pilot's phone and backpack in my crawl space, since our argument, we hadn't talked about the subject. We weren't separated, but we weren't together either. Not fighting, but much less at peace. With Moacir's death, things were in a state of suspension. I could very well have made it easier at the moment I left her at her house. Let's resolve this mess, I could have said, but I thought she'd ask for further explanations, and I didn't consider myself in any condition to offer them to anyone.

I unlocked the door and Sulamita came in. We embraced in silence for a long time. I smelled a pleasant fragrance in her hair. She looked pretty in a light-colored blue dress, loose-fitting and sheer, that slipped off her body when I undid the shoulder straps.

It was nothing special. A bit of fury in the heat, only that, and afterward silence, with my heart beating, racing.

And still later, a diffuse sadness, a mad desire to get out of there.

Later, in bed, smoking, I once again felt my head brimming with problems. And I said to Sulamita: You may not believe it, but Moacir was killed. And I don't want to die. I'm not going to die.

I said I had a plan in mind. A very good plan that would resolve my life. Our lives, I added. You can help me, I said. We can do this together and continue on our path. Take care of our family, the way we had dreamed. Of Regina and your parents. Of Serafina. But you can also turn it down. You can put on your clothes and leave. And never come back. But if you stay, you'll have to help me. Because I'm going ahead with it. With or without you, I'm going ahead with my plan.

That's what I told her.

Then she said:

When that damn cell phone rang in the crawl space, it turned my life upside down. You know me. I've always been well organized. I like things to be done right. I plan ahead for everything. And I do it by following rules. If rules exist, if there are laws, it's for people to have better lives, or so I imagine. In my opinion, order is everything. It wasn't by accident that I went to work for the police. I know: there's a lot of ingenuousness and idealism in that choice, we're not in Sweden, the police here are corrupt, but it's one thing to read about it in the papers and another to live and work like an honest person in a public agency. You know that corruption exists, but you don't see it. Corruption isn't something that comes from below. It has nothing to do with employees like me. You know everything's rotten, but you lead an honest life, with honest people who do their job.

And suddenly I find myself in the middle of an endless mess. Suddenly there's a missing pilot, cocaine, a huge debt in dollars, and I'm in the center of the confusion. And I love you. I left the house the day I discovered everything, and spent almost forty-eight hours off the air, not understanding a damn thing. All I could think about was "I love the guy." Until that day, you were the man in my life, and then I find out you're also some kind of trafficker. I asked myself what a sensible person should do in my situation and there weren't many answers. If I wanted to help, I ought to turn you in. The day Moacir died, even before learning it was a suicide, I realized I had to act quickly. Today it's Moacir, I thought, and tomorrow it may be my boyfriend. That's when I decided to ask for Joel's help, remember Joel? Tranqueira? I called Joel and said, Tranqueira, I really need to talk with you. I wanted to understand what was happening, to read the inquest papers on Moacir, to discuss it with Joel, tell him everything and, depending on the seriousness of the snafu, come here and persuade you to give yourself up. Joel is very good at giving advice and I know I can trust him. But Joel was in a meeting at that moment and asked me to come to the precinct later. And that's when the thing that wasn't supposed to happen happened. It has to do with God, I imagine. And with the telephone, too. It's strange how the telephone causes tragedy in people's lives nowadays. A part of our lives takes place over the phone, and it's also over the phone that people fuck themselves up. Joel didn't hang up properly and locked my line. At first I shouted, thinking he could hear me. But suddenly I began hearing their conversation. Besides Joel there was another person; I think it was Dudu, I'm not sure. They were putting the squeeze on a third person, the owner of a junkyard. From what I understood, the guy was caught red-handed distributing drugs and they were demanding a bribe to quash it then and there.

It's one thing to know the president is corrupt, the governor is corrupt, the secretary of security is corrupt. But the guy who's been working with you for seven years? Right beside you? Who has lunch and dinner with you? Who comes to your house? Joel? The one who taught me everything? I'd hold my hand over a flame for Joel. If Joel, Tranqueira, who calls me Sweetheart, is corrupt, if he's like that, then everyone in the precinct must be on the take. Nowadays there aren't any thieves without partners, corruption is a network, a pack. So why should I worry if my boyfriend steals a kilo of coke from someone who's already dead? Of course you shouldn't have gotten involved with Ramirez, but the truth is you haven't killed anybody. You haven't hurt anybody. You're not a murderer. Or a rapist. That's what matters. If you had taken someone's life, in that case there's no forgiving a homicide. But you're not a pedophile. Not that I condone what you did, but it's one thing to pick up a gun and kill, and another to do what you did. You're not a killer. That's why I'm here. Of course if you were arrested I could wait. But I'm already waited so damn long. I don't want to give up on our life or our plans. And our family needs us.

Now, she said, taking my hand, tell me about your plan.

23

My plan is like a fishing story. Imagine a solitary fisherman in his boat on a calm, sunny day. You know, there's everything in these Pantanal rivers. Truly horrible things. Otters and lizards so big they look like alligators. And alligators with sawtooth tails that resemble dragons. And piranhas that are miniature sharks with jaws that jut out and teeth as sharp as Swiss knives. And twenty-foot-long anacondas that can swallow an ox whole. Dreadful animals. Venomous. But the worst of all, the most threatening and dangerous, the most pitiless and predatory, is our solitary fisherman, who amuses himself on a sunny day. Really something awful. There he is, smoking a straw cigarette and thinking about life as he waits for some fish to take his bait. And suddenly he sees something caught in the branches of the vegetation. What is that? He approaches the right bank of the river and sees a body floating. Actually, it is what is left of the body of our pilot.

All of that, I continued, happened three months ago, when the accident and the pilot's disappearance in Corumbá was all over the news. The fisherman understands the deal immediately. He watched the reports on television and knows the accident took place in the vicinity. And his life is hard. He's unemployed and has no money. And he knows the Berabas. Who doesn't? Rich people from the city. And then, right there, while the sun bakes his brains, he concocts an incredible plan.

Sulamita, in bed, nude, her arms behind her head, listened to my plans, her eyes glued to me.

The jails are full of people with incredible plans, she said.

Imagine, I continued, that the fisherman recovers the body and buries it somewhere without telling anyone. Now, like in a film, you skip ahead in time. Three months later, the police have given up the search and things have calmed down. What does the fisherman do? He phones the Beraba family and says: I have the body of your son. If you want to bury him, all you have to do is pay me $200,000. And hangs up.

And are they going to pay? Sulamita asked.

They'll pay any amount, I guarantee it. Haven't you ever heard the saying "a man only begins to be a man when he buries his dead"? It's the gospel truth. There are no civilizations without death rituals. Without burials. Without them, we go back to the caves. Without them, you don't honor the deceased, his memory, you don't pay homage to him, you don't have a tomb to visit. We turn into zombies if we leave our dead to rot on the ground. On a personal level the tragedy is greater. I remember once on All Souls Day finding my mother crying in the kitchen and she said to me: "If at least there were a tomb for us to visit." My mother was suffering because my father had died. She was suffering because she couldn't declare that death.

Won't they involve the police?

No. Dona Lu will do whatever it takes to obtain the body.

You're pretty confident, she said.

"The dead kill the living," I replied, ever hear the saying?

You've got a lot of sayings.

Know what it means? Until we bury our dead, they go on living, killing us. That's what it means. They kill us by hammering at our awareness that we haven't done our part.

We don't allow them to return to dust. It's not only us, the living, who want to bury the dead. They themselves also want to be free of our world.

I explained that I really liked Dona Lu, truly. Believe me, I said, we won't be hurting her or her family, we're just going to let her hold her son's funeral. And $200,000 means nothing to those people. It's probably the cost of a single milk cow, and they've got thousands of them. We're going to kill three birds with one stone: she'll have her son's body, I'll have $50,000, and you'll realize your dream of leaving the morgue and having a ranch. All your own.

Our dream, she said.

Of course. Our plan. I'll pay Ramirez with the ransom and we'll buy a ranch.

You're going to bluff?

Bluff who?

The Berabas. Are you going to bluff or hand over the body?

That's where you come in. We have to provide a corpse.

Hmm. I know.

I'd really like to help Dona Lu's dream come true. To bury her son. Believe me, she dreams about the day. Dona Lu is a very good person. You'll like her.

We fell silent for a time, then I asked if she could get a cadaver from the morgue.

There's monitoring of the receiving and dispatching of bodies. It's not easy.

Without a body we have no plan.

Promise me one thing, she said. Whatever happens, we're not going to kill anybody.

We're not murderers.

I need some time to think.

There's got to be a way.

We're not murderers.

Of course not.

And if we do get a cadaver, it'll be just a cadaver, Sulamita said.

What do you mean?

It's not enough for Caesar's wife to be honest. She has to be above suspicion.

What're you saying? Who's Caesar?

We don't need merely a cadaver, any old cadaver. They have to believe it's Junior's cadaver. They'll want some guarantee that we have their son's cadaver.

You'll have to handle that too.

I asked whether we ran the risk of Junior's body turning up floating somewhere. The real body.

After three months? In this heat? she said. Hardly. My opinion is that he had his belly perforated. In drowning cases, if the belly is pierced the bodies sink and don't rise to the surface again.

I kissed Sulamita.

I knew you'd help me, I said.

Neither of us slept that night. Hour by hour I would raise a new question, a new detail. We spent the night like that. In the dark, full of ideas.

24

At eight in the morning I parked the van. Go by yourself, Sulamita said, it's better. I'll wait here. Leave the key, I'll stay in the car because of the air conditioning. And make it quick, try not to draw attention to yourself. Don't talk any more than necessary.

Leave it to me, I answered.

Before I got out, she pulled me to her. Give me a kiss, she said.

We kissed.

Tell me you love me.

I love you, I said.

A lot?

A lot.

How much?

Goddamn, Sulamita, let me take care of this business.

I got out of the car and walked to the pawnshop, which seemed like a cave in contrast to the light outside and the blue sky. It took me several seconds to get used to the darkness.

I came for my watch, I said.

The old man took my receipt, went to the back of the store, and soon returned with Junior's gold watch.

He wasn't very happy about it; those guys make their living out of our misfortune.

I paid and went back to the car.

Did he ask any questions? Sulamita wanted to know.

Nothing.

She looked at the watch. Pretty, she said. And it's running. I'm going to have to work on it too.

Ten minutes later I dropped Sulamita in front of the morgue.

We agreed to meet at home at nightfall.

The rest of the day was calm, except for an unpleasant encounter with Carlão when I went to the bank to pay the Berabas' bills. Carlão was with his ex-wife and looked like an obedient lapdog carrying the woman's purse, a red purse stuffed with baubles that didn't look good on the shoulder of that repentant brute. Actually, it was the ex, surely ignorant of the real reason for the separation of Carlão and Rita, who came to speak with me. Come over one of these days, she said, I'm taking back the restaurant at the gas station. Carlão looked at me with the same interest as a wooden stick. We need to see more of each other, she said, after all, you're cousins.

As soon as the woman took her eyes off me, he sent a signal: go fuck yourself, he said with that hairy hand of his.

When I got back to the Berabas', Dalva said Serafina was on the phone.

She threw me out, the Indian woman said.

Who are you talking about?

Eliana. She told me to find somewhere else to live.

I spoke with Dona Lu, asked for permission to leave early, and went to have a talk with Eliana.

If you're so worried about that Indian, she said without pausing from the grub she was preparing for the children, which judging by the smell I figured must be fried crow, if you're so worried, why don't you take her with you?

That's what I plan to do. But I need some time. For now, she doesn't have anywhere to go, I argued.

Yes she does, that tribe in the middle of nowhere. All she has to do is get her stuff and leave. The government pays for those people to go back.

You don't feel sorry for your mother-in-law?

Mother-in-law? That good-for-nothing? And when did Moacir ever feel sorry for me? Or our children? Did he leave any money to pay my bills?

How much do you need?

For what?

To pay your bills.

Eliana's expression showed her displeasure.

How much do you want? I asked.

Five hundred.

I took out my wallet and gave her everything I had. I'll get the rest, I said. But you're going to have to keep Serafina until I get my life organized.

I turned my back and left.

A tramp, Eliana. And to think that because of her Moacir fucked up his life.

So far, so good, over. I'm safe inside my house and there's no ill wind here. Or rain. Good weather, everything in its place, over. Everything's going to work out. That was my thought as I watched a TV program about tornadoes.

Sulamita arrived at seven and stayed beside me, her legs in my lap. The images on TV were impressive: barns, cars, fence posts being sucked up by an invisible pump. It looks like some special effect, Sulamita said. We remained there, in bed, holding hands, feeling protected while we talked about how those people, the owners of cars and houses, the inhabitants of those cities, were fucked. Other people's misfortunes, she said, are a form of entertainment, don't you think? Fun to watch, I added.

That's disgusting, we agreed. They do it to sell stuff, I said. And it sells, we agreed. They sell because we buy.

After the program, Sulamita turned off the television and suggested we go out for a pizza.

I didn't want to leave; I felt vulnerable and couldn't stop looking to all sides, behind me, all the time scared of taking a bullet to the head.

If Ramirez gave you a month to pay off the debt, Sulamita said in the pizzeria, he's not going to kill you like that, suddenly, what Ramirez wants is the fifty thousand. It doesn't make sense to kill you ahead of time.

I agreed with Sulamita's arguments, but that didn't keep me from looking all around me. We should sit with our backs to the wall, I said. And we moved to a table in the rear.

During the meal, she showed me Junior's watch. Dirty, scratched, and broken. We had talked a lot the night before about the type of proof we should offer.

We have to take into account that the watch was in the water until the fisherman found the cadaver. That's how we talked, about the fisherman, as if it were some other person, over, and not ourselves doing it.

You think of everything, I said.

Where is Junior's cell phone? she asked.

I had brought it but said I didn't know if it was a good idea to use it. Follow my thinking. We're assuming the backpack wasn't with Junior at the moment of the rescue, therefore neither was the telephone. Besides which, if it was, the phone would be broken because it would have been in the water for several hours.

You're right, she said, but if they have caller ID the number that shows will be Junior's.

Of course, I said, kissing Sulamita. Logic be damned.

After dinner, we crossed the Jacaré Bridge and parked in a quiet spot as if we were going to make out.

Use this, she said, handing me the flannel cloth from my van's glove box. And disguise your voice.

Wouldn't it be better for you to talk?

No, she said. The fisherman has to be a man.

I dialed, and Dalva answered.

I'd like to talk to Dona Lourdes Beraba, I said in a deep voice.

Who's calling?

A friend, I replied.

Seconds later I heard Dona Lu's gentle, receptive voice. Who is it? Hello?

I hesitated for an instant. Then I spoke.

I have your son's body with me. Don't call the police. You'll receive instructions. If you involve the police you'll never hear from me again, I said.

I hung up. Or rather, the fisherman hung up.

It was that simple.

25

I didn't want to go on feeling like that all the time. Hunted, a deer running in an open field. A rabbit in frightened flight. Ramirez couldn't make another mistake. I always paid everything, I mean. I'm a reliable payer, one of those who can't sleep when they owe something. A trait inherited from my mother, actually. That was our religion, to pay everything on time. Debt was a kind of sin in our house.

On the veranda of his factory in Puerto Suárez, Ramirez didn't even look at me. He was more interested in his brand-new black Mitsubishi parked in the garage. Stolen probably, over. In the living room some people, maybe more swallowers of cocaine capsules, were talking with Juan.

Sulamita had told me that people line up for that kind of work and that at the precinct she'd seen women with bundles of drugs the size of a tennis ball in their pussy.

It's not good business to kill me, over. You're going to lose fifty grand. Lose a partner. I was there to say that, had come very early, without phoning, which didn't sit well with them. I'm gonna give you a tip, Porco: we don't like surprises around here, Juan had said. But I had to straighten out the situation. Make a pact with Ramirez. An oath. I swear it, I was going to say. My legs were shaking, I was panting like a dog and couldn't get out even a sentence of the speech I had rehearsed in the car en route to Puerto Suárez. All I said was shit, lies, while hearing my internal radio, over, saying I was about to fuck myself up. I told him about Moacir and how he'd been found in his cell. And how he'd belched when they removed the sheet he had used to hang himself. The final sigh of the hanged, I said. If you're strangled, I said, not understanding why I was going down that crooked road, you don't belch. And you don't ejaculate, isn't that interesting? They told me Moacir had a hard-on when he was found. Covered in cum. And I laughed as if that was funny.

Porco says the damnedest things, said Ramirez. You running some angle?

Huh?

You got something special to tell me?

No, it's that Moacir –

I don't give a shit about Moacir, Ramirez interrupted.

I'm going to pay, I said. You don't have to worry about me.

Ramirez guffawed. I'm absolutely sure you're going to pay, he replied.

Then he yelled to Juan, Bring me my notebook.

Juan left the house and returned a short time later with a large book with a black cover, the kind accountants used in the past.

That's how these guys get screwed, I thought, by keeping spreadsheets like the CEO of a multinational. And now my name was there among all the other traffickers.

It's written here, Ramirez said. Porco, sixty thousand dollars. You're Porco, ain't you?

Yes, I said.

Okay then, you already know.

You had said fifty, I ventured.

I did? And even so, you come here to jerk my chain? Now you know, it's sixty, he said, making the change in the book.

He paused before adding the rest.

Every time you come to my house with bullshit, I'm adding ten thousand dollars to what you owe.

He added that I had twenty-four days to settle the debt. And that I ought to consider the grace period a goodwill gesture. I ain't usually so generous.

Driving back to downtown Puerto Suárez, I was overcome by a sense of relief. After all, I had 24 days, over. Better than twenty-four hours. If Ramirez said twenty-four days, I had twenty-four days. Earlier, I'd had thirty, and now twenty-four. Which was fair, if you consider the size of the debt. Sixty grand. And ten kilos of cocaine.

I couldn't stop thinking that this was how someone condemned to death must feel. Twenty-four days. His quota and then the electric chair. And kidney cancer too. The doctor says: six months. A deadline and it's over. My advantage is that I had the reprieve, the antidote, right there in my pocket. Sulamita had prepared everything that morning: a small wooden box with Junior's watch, to be mailed to the Berabas from there, Puerto Suárez.

Sulamita had carefully cleaned the watch, removing our fingerprints, and wrapped it in carbon paper, a technique to thwart X-rays.

We also took care to write the name of the recipient on a sticker printed on Sulamita's computer and to use a fake return address. If they checked, they'd quickly see the street and the number didn't exist.

I parked two blocks from the post office and walked, avoiding the puddles, over, feeling the volume of the package in the pocket of my jeans jacket.

Movement was heavy work. A luncheonette, trinket store, bank, another trinket store, bakery, yet another trinket store, all packed because of the rain, which was coming down harder now.

I hesitated in front of the post office, not knowing whether to go in or ask someone to do it for me. A kid, one of those who offers to carry tourists' bags, could handle it. Don't trust anyone, over. Then a group of American backpackers went into the agency, creating the kind of confusion typical of adolescents. I joined them and mailed the watch, not drawing much attention to myself.

Mission accomplished, I thought as I got into the car.

26

The next few days were days of waiting.

The fisherman didn't get in contact, but there was tension in the house that you could feel in the air.

The three times I spoke with Dona Lu, I noticed that she kept the cell phone in her hand the entire time. And if it rang, she didn't wait for the second ring and answered it with an anxiety that I knew very well.

I remember that my mother once went to take a bath and asked me to listen for the phone. I ended up falling asleep and awoke to hear her yelling, fallen on the floor, wrapped in a towel, crying. Why didn't you answer? she screamed.

At the Berabas' I also witnessed the moment when the rancher, returning from work, asked his wife if they had called. Nothing, she said. Nothing yet.

On another day, when I went in to deliver their mail, I found Dona Lu sleeping in the living room, with the phone in her lap. She was rapidly losing weight and no longer seemed to care about the white roots of her hair, which contrasted greatly with the dyed part. She had completely lost any vanity. She wore a faded blue robe and mustard-colored slippers. She looked like an old flower. With no fragrance. My presence woke her; she straightened up on the sofa and said she was doing that lately, sleeping anywhere. And at night, she said, I stay awake. She asked if I had brothers or sisters. I said no. You're like Junior, she said. An only child. And her eyes welled with tears. I felt such love for Dona Lu that day that, if there had been any other way to get the money, I would have aborted the plan. There is no other way, over.

She's hanging on by a thread, said Dalva in the kitchen. Now she only drinks milk. Nothing else.

Early Wednesday morning, the bomb exploded. As soon as the package that I had mailed from Puerto Suárez came, it was as if an alarm had gone off. José Beraba was informed by phone, and half an hour later parked his car in the garage. Dona Lu's doctor also arrived hurriedly.

What's happening? Dalva asked.

Later, I was called to Mr. José's office. He asked if I was the one who had received the mail that morning.

I said yes.

Was it the same mailman as always?

The same, I said. Is there some problem?

No, he said, dismissing me.

In the kitchen, before I left, Dalva offered me a slice of the orange cake she had just baked. Something's going on, she said. Something very strange. Have you noticed it? It was after you took them the mail, Dalva said.

That night, I told Sulamita everything.

We're getting into Phase B of our plan, she said.

Sulamita had heard that an effective pressure technique used by kidnappers was to phone the family and, instead of making demands or threats, simply remain silent. Silence, she said, is a horrible threat. We have to destabilize them. We have to shake them up. We have to prevent them from moving.

For a long time, I believed that evil was a slow learning process. In those days, however, I finally understood that kindness is learned with great difficulty, through daily exercises that people sometimes call God or Buddha, depending on their beliefs. We are born with evil ensconced in us like a dormant virus only waiting for the moment to emerge. Otherwise, how to explain my behavior and Sulamita's? How to explain that two good people could act so horribly?

There was no trace in Sulamita of the terrified woman of a few days before. It was she who thought of the details and made the decisions. Maybe because of that my internal radio, that voice inside me, spoke less now. It still spoke, but with gaps and interference. It no longer guided me. It just alerted. It was Sulamita who was in charge.

Getting back to what matters: our nights were long studies of probability. At times it was as if we were in a frenetic ghost train running off the tracks, as if that grotesque plan were a dark adventure that awoke a savage tremor in us. Sulamita's eyes glowed with excitement. And mine burned. We have to study every detail, she said. Especially the cadaver. And the money. I would wake up in the middle of the night, think about this too, I remembered. And about that. And I slept and she would awaken me. One mistake, one single mistake and we're fucked, she repeated. You know, she said, it's like a game of chess. And she would ask questions for which I had no answer. The color of Junior's hair and eyes, his height and weight. How am I supposed to know? I asked. Checkmate, she said. Find out. I need precise information. Think. Remember. How do you expect me to come up with a cadaver if I don't even know Junior's height?

The same night that the package was delivered, the fisherman phoned the family. We repeated the calls at various times on following days. Sulamita also phoned a few times while I was at work, so they wouldn't suspect me.

Late Friday night I called four times. Dona Lu or Mr. José answered, in great distress, begging the fisherman to say something. You're using our son's phone, they said.

137

The fisherman made no sound, only breathing. A heavy breathing, rhythmical like that of an unhurried animal waiting for the right moment to attack – that's how I felt on the other end of the line.

The last time, Mr. José lost control.

You cur, he said. You worm. You son of a bitch.

And hung up in my face.

27

The sun shone in through the spaces between the roof tiles. And also through the sides, the cracks, and under the door.

It was Saturday, I was in bed, half asleep, half awake. The ceiling fan was humming, but even so I could hear the laughter. It seemed like a crackling fire. Through the window glass I could see the tops of heads. I was even pleased by the sight. A bunch of nosy half-pints. The children were guffawing. Whispering. Climb on the roof, one of them said. I knew what they wanted. I got up slowly and opened the window, howling threats. They ran away laughing, in a band. They'd be back, I knew, hoping I'd play the game again.

Outside, the day was hot. Serafina was washing the sidewalk with the hose. I'll make you some fresh coffee, she said when she saw me.

At eight, Sulamita called. She was irritated at her father. The old man's hopeless, she said. I found out he bought the neighbor's VW and I had to cancel the deal, can you believe it?

I asked about the preparations, and she said everything was ready. Come pick me up, she said.

As I was coming out of the shower, Serafina knocked at the door and handed me a cup of coffee along with a brown envelope with no return address. It arrived yesterday, she said.

I noticed she had a bruise on her arm. What's that? I asked.

She smiled awkwardly.

Was it Eliana?

No, she answered, not looking away. I bumped into the wardrobe.

Eliana mustn't do that, do you understand?

Serafina went downstairs, taking the empty coffee cup.

I opened the envelope and found a kind of X-ray. On it was a red tag in the form of an arrow pointing to a tiny spot on the image. On the attached sheet was the following information: Ultrasound examination. Placenta with 9 mm fetus. The arrow indicates the blood-suffused heart.

Only that, nothing else. It was postmarked Rio de Janeiro. So was that where Rita had gone?

I stood there, looking at that black sheet, out of breath. The dot. Rio de Janeiro. I burned everything and went downstairs to speak with Serafina. I asked her to never give me anything in front of Sulamita. You promise?

Yes, she said.

It's very important. Do you understand?

Yes, she repeated.

I got in the car and started thinking about what I had just seen. It was just a dot, but it already had a heart and blood.

The beggar was sleeping on a steaming tombstone, the sun hitting him in the face. No one else was around. Only dogs and trash.

We walked down the fetid passageways of the cemetery, Sulamita carrying the bouquet of wildflowers we had bought en route. If anything comes up, she said, we're visiting the tomb of my paternal grandmother.

We were holding hands. I was sweating profusely and looking behind me at every moment. The sun was intense.

If they're following us, I said, they're going to catch us.

Nobody's watching us, Sulamita replied.

I trust you, I said, looking back again.

Sulamita stopped in front of a ravaged sepulcher from which emanated a strong smell of urine.

Your behavior isn't helping, she said. Try to control yourself. You're just making me more nervous.

The day was clear, without a single cloud, and I felt I lacked the strength to go on walking under that sun.

Are you afraid? she asked.

It's a horrible thing we're doing, I answered.

We're not going to kill anyone, she said. Think about your mother. About Dona Lu. You said yourself that she's going to feel better once all this is over.

We were at the stage in the plan where we were starting to spend money. Sulamita's money. That week, I had offered to sell the van. No way, she had said. We can't do anything that draws attention – selling, buying, spending, fighting, separating, nothing. Not now and not later, when everything is over. You're going to have to go on working at the Berabas' for a good period of time. As if nothing had happened. Know when a criminal messes up?

We're not murderers, I had said.

Of course not, she had replied, but we are committing a crime. And there's one guideline for people who do what we're doing: don't change your routine, it's when you change your routine that we, the police, find the thread.

I'm thinking about your money, I said. The money you're going to spend. Think about it. If we're going to back out, it has to be now, I said.

I don't want to back out of anything, she replied. I have friends who drink before going to work. You might want to have something to drink too. It would calm you down. Now let's go on, she said, pulling me by the hand. He's waiting for us.

The man's name was Gilmar. His suntanned body and his earth-stained clothes were a kind of blot on that luminous day. He was holding a hoe in one hand and his hat in the other.

We were in the middle of the cemetery, with horseflies buzzing around us. On the way, Sulamita had told me that the place had been taken over by vandals. The sepulchers and mausoleums serve as latrines for beggars, she had said. The government is authorized to open the resting places of those buried more than five years, but thieves and tramps open them and take what they want, she had stated.

Now she was talking to Gilmar, and I stayed at a distance, as if that way I wouldn't be part of the macabre negotiation.

It's been five months, Gilmar said.

That's not a problem, Sulamita answered. As long as it's a man.

It's a man, he said. I buried him myself.

What's the height?

Five-eleven, just like you asked for.

How do we do it? she asked.

I'll dig him up today and you come by tonight. I'll be waiting at the gate.

There's no watchman? she asked.

Gilmar laughed.

While they talked about payment, I couldn't think about anything but that dark spot. That red arrow. 9 mm. Placenta.

What if I were in Rio with Rita? I closed my eyes and imagined the scene, the two of us holding hands as we walked along the beach. Hang gliders in the sky, a breeze cooling our bodies. Let's go swimming, said Rita. And we plunged into the water.

Soaked in sweat, we left the cemetery. The sun was merciless.

28

Half an hour later, when I parked in front of the construction supply store, Sulamita handed me the list.

> 2 raincoats
> 2 pairs of gloves
> 2 goggles
> 2 masks
> 1 hoe
> 8 meters of thick black plastic
> 1 blowtorch
> 1 hammer
> 2 strong flashlights
> 8 hundred-liter garbage bags
> 5 meters of black canvas
> Rope

Buy the first four items here and leave the rest for other stores, she said, handing me the money she had withdrawn from her savings the day before.

The fact that Sulamita was bankrolling the operation also bothered me.

We're going to recoup what we're spending, I said.

She kissed me.

I got out of the car, made the purchases, and we repeated the procedure in three more stores in the city in order to avoid drawing attention to ourselves. When I returned to the car after buying the last of the materials, I found Sulamita on the sidewalk.

What is it? I asked.

I wanted to make sure we weren't being followed.

I looked around us, frightened.

It was just a check, she said. I thought I saw Joel. But it's clear.

We got in the car, me with my eye on the rearview mirror.

What now? I asked.

Now I want something to eat. I'm starving.

You know, my father-in-law said, that I'm going to pay you. He was speaking softly, afraid that Sulamita would hear us. We had just had lunch and were sitting in front of the TV, watching some idiotic film. I should have cut the conversation short, Talk to your daughter, I should have said, she's the one who can solve your problem. But I let the old man ramble on. The thing is, he said, that I lent money to a friend and I don't want to pressure my friend, you know? Money puts an end to friendships, he said. If I press him, I'll lose the friendship and a good friend is hard to find. It's different than owing somebody in your own family. Like us. I owe you, but I'm going to pay. And if someday you need it, I can give you a loan. In the future. And you'll pay me when you can. I'll never dun my own son-in-law. But I'm going to pay you. I need you to lend me another thousand. Twelve hundred, actually. My friend's going to pay me, and I'll use it to pay you. I'll pay the five plus the thousand you're going to lend me now.

I noticed that Regina was paying attention to her father and smiling at me. Then she looked at her father again and gave an odd guffaw, like pebbles falling to the ground. The old man went on talking, and every time he repeated that he would pay me, Regina threw more pebbles on the ground. And looked at me. I found that funny and began to laugh too.

Stop that, Regina, said the old man. But then he realized what was happening and began laughing with us. A real pistol, that girl, he said. Nothing retarded about her. She's just a bit off. We laugh a lot. People think she's crafty, he said, choking on his own laughter, but she's keeping her eye on us.

And the three of us were laughing our heads off when Sulamita arrived and asked what was so funny.

That retard is very clever, said her father, still laughing.

Sulamita became furious when Regina was referred to that way. Don't talk like that, she said. Such ignorance, father. She's not retarded. And the quarrel began. The daughter yelled at the old man, who yelled at his daughter, who yelled at her mother and father, who yelled at each other, making Regina cry. I had witnessed the scene several times. Now do you understand why I can't leave home? she asked. They don't know how to take care of my sister.

Let's take Regina for some ice cream, Sulamita said. Help me get her into the car.

Late in the day, after leaving Regina with her parents, we went to my place and took a bath. Put on old clothes, said Sulamita, who had done the same minutes before at her house.

The sun had set less than half an hour earlier. We had time and decided to have a pizza at a place with outdoor tables where you could feel the breeze from the river.

The restaurant was packed with families and children, and I felt at ease, especially once the vodka began to take effect.

We ate and went on drinking, killing time.

Sulamita told me that when she was in college her anatomy professor recommended a story about murder and the sale of cadavers, based on events that occurred in London in the nineteenth century. A sordid story: amoral people who suffocated beggars and sold their bodies to the universities. But all that sordidness, she said, had a noble purpose, which was science and progress. The story, she continued, was by Robert Louis Stevenson and was called "The Body Snatcher."

After saying this, she fell silent for several instants.

We don't even have a noble purpose, she said, with an expression of vulnerability.

We were like that now, with one or the other always thinking about giving up our gruesome plan. First me, then her. Afterward me again, and her once more. And then both of us together. Or just her. Just me. Day after day like that, an infernal seesaw.

I realized that Sulamita couldn't drink anymore. I took the glass from her hand, telling the waiter that I wanted to take the bottle of vodka with me.

But I'm the only one who's going to drink, advised Sulamita. You don't have the stomach for it.

At eleven that night we arrived at the cemetery. Gilmar was at the gate with a woman who I later learned was his wife. Lots of people make a living that way, Sulamita explained. They sell everything: objects, vases, and even the bronze plaques from the tombs.

As we followed the couple in the dark, the smell of rot entered through the car's window.

What if they talk?

There's no way to be involved in a plan like this without leaving skin on the barbed wire. We've got to take the chance, she said.

Do you trust him?

We're paying well. That's what I trust. Money.

When we arrived at the farthest confines of the cemetery, Gilmar motioned for us to stop.

When I got out of the car I saw a modest coffin sitting beside a simple grave.

How are we going to carry it? I asked.

Get the canvas out of the car, Sulamita replied.

I kept my back turned while the couple opened the coffin, only hearing Sulamita's instructions to wrap the corpse and put it in the bed of the van.

We had brought black plastic to seal off the body of the vehicle.

I got back into the car when everything was ready and waited for Sulamita to pay the couple.

It was twenty-past eleven when we left the cemetery.

29

We drove for over half an hour on the dirt road without meeting a soul. Sulamita knew the route well. At the next entrance, she said, park near the fence. It's an old abandoned farm. No one ever comes to these parts.

My head was spinning from the vodka.

We parked, and when I turned off the lights it was as if night had plummeted onto our heads. I couldn't even see my own hands.

I turned on the headlights, drank a bit more vodka, and we got out, taking with us the materials we had brought on the rear seat of the van.

Then I turned on the flashlights and Sulamita handed me the raincoat, the goggles, the boots, and gloves for me to get ready. While she was getting dressed, she told me of a disease caused by necrophagous worms that caused blindness. Careful, she said.

We removed the body from the van and placed it on the ground.

We had agreed that I would dig the grave while she prepared the cadaver. But because of the darkness she thought it better for us to do everything together. You have to bring the light close to him, she said.

Sulamita was on her knees in front of the car, taking advantage of the illumination from the headlights. I approached with the flashlights, and it was only then that I saw the body.

Nothing was recognizable; there was a kind of gelatinous mass, a slime covering the skeleton. Every hair on my body stood on end from fear.

Anxiously, I drank more vodka. Sulamita too.

Pieces of rotting clothing still clung to the body.

Using scissors, Sulamita cut away the remaining cloth and put it in a garbage bag. She performed a meticulous search to make sure there were no identifying objects.

Then I dug a deep hole and we carefully placed the body inside, removing the black canvas we had used to transport it.

Just when I thought the worst was past, Sulamita asked me to point the light into the grave. With the hammer she broke the teeth and legs of the deceased in several places. They won't be able to establish the identity from dental records. I've done autopsies on pilots who died in crashes, she said. They're all smashed up. She took the blowtorch and charred the skeleton's legs.

Then we closed the grave, gathered the canvas and the plastic bags, and lit a bonfire.

The goggles, hoe, and all the other objects were tossed in the river in a garbage bag weighted down with stones.

At three in the morning we arrived at my house.

We went directly into the bathroom, turned on the shower, and remained silent, embracing, feeling the water cascade over us.

On Sunday, when Sulamita arose, I had already put the clothes we had worn the night before into a garbage bag. We're going out, I said.

We had breakfast at the corner bakery and then left on the Old Highway. After leaving the city, we stopped at a dump and got rid of our clothes.

We spent the morning swimming in the same grotto that we always went to. We practically didn't speak.

Sulamita told me several times that she loved me.

We lay in the sun, drying our bodies. I was so tired that at times I closed my eyes and slept.

One of those times, I awoke with Sulamita looking at me.

She asked me if we would someday forget what we had done.

I sighed.

What I fear, she said, is that we'll carry that cadaver for the rest of our lives.

We'll have to carry something, I thought. But I didn't say anything. I closed my eyes and went on feeling the sun on my body.

30

When I arrived at work on Monday, Dalva already knew everything. She confessed without embarrassment that she had eavesdropped on her employers' conversation through the door. You know, she said while she served me fresh coffee, I've been in this house for over twenty years. I raised that boy. I have the right to know what's going on.

Breathing heavily, she pulled up a stool and sat in front of me.

Remember that crazy guy who called here saying that Junior was dead? He's still calling, she said.

I felt my heart race. Stay calm, over. They don't know anything, over. I remembered what Sulamita had said about her profession, after we buried the body. Maybe now you understand, she said, the shame I feel at working in the morgue. People are disgusted by me. They avoid speaking to me, as if I could contaminate them. And the worst part is that I do feel contaminated.

While Dalva told me about the mysterious calls the Berabas had been receiving for several days, I also felt infected.

Do you think it's possible to kidnap a corpse? asked Dalva. From what I understood, they kidnapped Junior's body. I didn't know that now they kidnap cadavers. That's new to me. How can they kidnap a cadaver?

Dalva was confused: it was as if she were telling me, Okay, I understand criminals killing, raping, stealing, kidnapping, demanding ransoms, I understand them slaughtering and burning, blowing up the World Trade Center, but stealing cadavers? Bodies aren't stolen, that's what she meant. Cadavers exist to be buried in cemeteries.

Actually, over, I wasn't hearing what Dalva was saying any longer, just staring at her puzzled face and repeating to myself that at least we hadn't killed anyone. We're not murderers, I repeated silently, and when I focused my attention on Dalva again, I confirmed my earlier predictions: Mr. José wanted to call the police and Dona Lu was against it. They're arguing all the time, Dalva said.

She told me further that Dona Lu was wearing Junior's watch. You know, she said, I think Mr. José is right. They should call the police. If I got my hands on a lowlife like that, I don't know what I'd do. To me anybody who does that kind of thing deserves to die in the electric chair. It's a real shame Brazil doesn't have the death penalty.

After breakfast I felt worse. I became nauseous and went into the bathroom to vomit. I had woken up that morning feeling sick, but Sulamita insisted I mustn't change my routine. At a time like this, she said, anything irregular is suspect.

I vomited twice more undetected. To outward appearances, I was calm.

Dalva kept coming to me in the garage with unusual questions. How did the criminals get hold of Junior's body? Were they in the plane? Or did they find Junior dead after the accident? And where did they keep the body, in a refrigerator? Why didn't they kidnap Junior alive? Junior alive must be worth a lot more money than Junior dead, she said.

There came a moment when the questions grew more heated. Doesn't your girlfriend work at the morgue? What does she do exactly? Can she tell, looking at a cadaver, that it's really Junior's? Or if it's another person? Are there tests for that?

It was obvious, I thought; of course they would make the association. You're going to get caught, over. I called Sulamita several times. Keep calm, she told me, don't ruin everything. You have to stay calm, that's all. No one knows anything. Isn't that what Dalva said?

After lunch, Mr. José called me into his office.

When I entered, he was talking on the phone to one of his ranch hands and gestured for me to wait.

I observed the wilted hibiscuses outside the window. They hadn't even bloomed and were already dead. That was life in Corumbá.

Dalva told me your girlfriend works for the police, he said, hanging up the phone.

I confirmed the information. And on impulse asked if there was anything we could do to help.

He looked at me, thinking of the best way to tell me what must be said.

Then Dona Lu came into the office. It's impressive what pain can do to people. The damage is greatest in the face. When I looked at that defeated woman, the sound of Sulamita breaking the bones of the cadaver, a sharp sound almost like a crack, was ringing in my ears.

Lu, the rancher said, his fiancée works for the police.

I know, she said.

She looked at her husband and then at me, distressed, as if fearing some piece of bad news. Then in her gentle way she asked me to leave them by themselves.

They spoke loudly; I couldn't help but hear. I stopped in the middle of the living room, hearing everything they said. Dalva came in with a tray of coffee and stood beside me. Listen to what I'm going to say, Dona Lu said. I want

154

my son. I have the right to bury my son, she said. I'm going to bury my son even if it's the last thing I do on earth. And you're not going to stand in my way. She repeated this several times amid sobs. And she cried, imploring her husband to listen, not to take a stance, not to call the police, not to ask anyone for help. Including me. Because nothing that could be done, however well it might be done, would bring Junior back. Even if the police discovered who the mentally ill person blackmailing them was, Junior would still be dead. And she would rather die than not bury her own son.

After that, we heard nothing but her crying, which was neither sobs nor moans but only the phrase "I want my son," intoned like a prayer or mantra.

I saw that Dalva was crying too. I myself had a knot in my throat. I took her to the kitchen and went into the bathroom to vomit again. It had been horrific to witness that scene, but on the other hand I felt safer. They're not going to alert the police, I thought.

That day I made five trips to the pharmacy to buy medicines for Dona Lu. The doctor came to see her and spent the afternoon at the house.

At six, I met Sulamita at the entrance to the morgue. I told her what had happened, in detail.

You're sure that was all? she asked.

Yes.

He didn't ask anything further about my work?

No, and I didn't say anything. There wasn't time. Dona Lu interrupted our conversation. But Dalva asked questions. Maybe Dalva suspects, I don't know. She also asked about my life in São Paulo. But maybe it's nothing.

We were in the car, and the heat was making me dizzy.

What about him? Mr. José? Think he suspects you? asked Sulamita.

I've changed my opinion on that several times during the day, I replied. I've thought yes and no. Sometimes I think everything is so obvious. You, the morgue. On the other hand, I know how these things go. When you're in the middle of it, suffering, you can't have an overall view of the situation. When I think about my mother, for example, I believe he would come to me for help. That's all.

Rich the way he is? Why doesn't he ask the secretary of public security for help?

Because Dona Lu wants to bury her son. Because the police can get in the way. They might scare off the kidnapper.

She's not going to alert the police?

No. You can take that to the bank.

We had talked about it a lot. Sulamita believed the problem might arise in the future. There are moments, she said, when they'll have to bring in the police. When they receive the body. They'll have to do a DNA test for the burial. It's normal procedure. The police will ask questions.

However, Sulamita knew a worker in the Brasilia laboratory where the tests in the region were carried out. She believed we could convince him to help us.

How? I asked.

For six hundred, she said. You can convince a guy to do anything for six hundred. All you have to do is pay.

Now, she said, the important thing is to use the strategy of silence. We're going to terrorize them. We're going to disappear for a time. Silence is our most powerful weapon.

31

When you commit a crime like this the problem isn't the others. Much less the reality. The evidence. The problem is you yourself. The slip-up you make when you're asked a question. The imperfect actions. Your inappropriate reaction in a given situation. Not to mention the urge to confess that arises time and again. That's common, said Sulamita. Guilt is the feeling that usually leads to fatal consequences at such moments. People simply don't take into account the extra weight they begin to carry. They want to be free of it so they can sleep. Actually, confession has more to do with relief than with repentance. It functions like a salve. A discharge. Afterward, people repent having confessed, but then it's too late.

Our conversations in bed were always about such matters. How we should act in this or that situation. Self-control is the watchword, Sulamita said. Permanent self-control.

I had relapses, but in general I did all right. It didn't matter what Dalva asked or what happened at the house. I remained firm until we decided the moment had come.

On a Monday, around nine in the evening, we went to the neighborhood square, taking Junior's cell phone.

The first call was tense. They wanted to know why their son's phone was still working: Didn't you say you found my son in the water? They were quite nervous, and I took advantage of that. I said they had ample proof, that the mere fact of me talking to them from that number was one more piece of evidence, and that we wanted $200,000 to hand over the cadaver.

I don't have that amount, stated José Beraba. And I don't even know for sure that you're telling the truth.

In less than two hours I called back twice. I threatened, said that if they called the police they would never learn how to find their son.

Later, as we had ice cream in the square, I summarized the conversations for Sulamita.

The rich are goddamn tough, she said. Even at times like this they want to bargain.

The night was stuffy, and on the way home we decided to buy a bottle of vodka. Sulamita also bought chocolates, peanuts, and potato chips.

We stayed at home the rest of the night, watching a science fiction film muted. At times, groggy from the vodka, I managed to doze off. And would wake up immediately, with a start, a sharp sound in my ear, like the crack of a whip.

When the cracking stopped, I fell into a heavy sleep and dreamed of Rita. I had a load of explanations to give; I was ready to ask forgiveness, but Rita only wanted to show me that damn sonogram. See this spot here? she asked. I couldn't see anything. It's our child, she said. And suddenly we were fucking like two dogs, in the cemetery where Sulamita and I had bought the cadaver. You can come inside me, she said.

I awoke with my orgasm, feeling terrible. Sulamita wasn't in the bed.

When I went into the bathroom, I found her in the shower. I haven't slept a wink, she said. I saw she'd been crying.

I took off my clothes, got into the shower, and we started kissing. She licked my neck, went on kissing me, and I thought I wouldn't have the strength for fucking at that moment.

When I came it was slow, weak, like an echo.

The next morning, when we left for work, I heard Eliana bellowing. I was irritated at the widow and knew exactly what was going on in that hole.

I asked Sulamita to wait for me in the car.

When I entered Eliana's kitchen I found Serafina sitting by the Formica table, with one of the grandchildren protecting her from their mother's fury.

I took Eliana outside to talk.

I didn't let her say a word. You see Sulamita over there? I asked, pointing to the van. She's got her eye on you. She wants me to warn you: if you lay a hand on Serafina again, she's coming here to arrest you, understand? You know what the penalty is for mistreating Indians? I'm giving you notice, it's a crime without bail. Worse than trafficking drugs or rare birds, you hear me?

She stared at me, not knowing what to say.

Sulamita waved at us from the car.

When I drove away, Sulamita asked if there was some problem.

Not at all, I said.

We're going to the bank, Beraba said as soon as he got in the car.

The day's beginning well, I thought while I waited in the car. Some moments later he returned, accompanied by the manager, who was carrying a black valise like the ones you see in the movies, to transport the money.

159

At four o'clock Dona Lu asked me to go with her to the church. She seemed more willing than her husband, and said she was receiving grace and wished to give thanks. I saw she wanted to talk, but I only managed to say yes and no, unable to come up with anything resembling conversation. On the way back, she kept her eyes closed, holding a rosary. I saw that she never stopped praying.

My stomach still wasn't in good shape, and as the day progressed I became more and more nauseated. I was careful, however, to maintain my composure.

That night, I did what Sulamita and I had agreed on.

At seven o'clock I phoned and spoke with José Beraba. I agreed to reduce the ransom to the figure he proposed: $160,000.

In the men's room at the airport, I said, under the sink, you'll find the instructions. Go alone. And I hung up.

Afterward, I went to meet Sulamita at the precinct.

She had bought a strawberry pie and gone to visit old friends.

We're engaged, she said when I arrived.

We received congratulations. The entire squad was there, and we didn't notice anything unusual.

Later, Sulamita invited Joel to have dinner with us. Dudu, the chief's sycophant, with his aged Weimaraner's face, also came along.

It was a gathering full of stories I had already heard, which they loved telling again, like the day Sulamita had slapped a young guy who was giving a statement, a rapist who was mocking us, she said. The bastard was talking and laughing, Sulamita continued, as if it was funny raping poor little girls.

Just as he was about to confess, Joel added, this crazy woman here gets up from the computer and slaps him. The chief felt like killing her, said Joel, guffawing.

On the way home, Sulamita told me that the Berabas were living up to their part of the bargain. The police don't know anything, she said. You saw it with your own eyes.

All clear, over.

32

Seven in the morning.

At the bakery, we ordered coffee and bread with butter.

The chances of getting away with theft are almost a hundred percent, said Sulamita. And if you kill someone, there's only a fifteen percent probability of getting caught. These are statistics from a study in Rio de Janeiro, she said, showing me the newspaper.

I was nervous, and Sulamita was trying to calm me down. But she was worse than me, and I had to calm her as well.

If Rio is like that, I stated, in the rest of Brazil it's far worse. Corumbá isn't even Brazil; we're practically in Bolivia.

Keep your voice down, she said. The problem is that we're not just stealing.

But we're not killing, I argued. We haven't killed anybody.

Keep your voice down, she repeated. The issue, she said, ignoring my arguments, is that we're selling a false cadaver to one of the richest families in Corumbá.

The ransom was the most sensitive part of our plan. Sulamita had set the details, always considering that the police could be alerted. I'm a cop, she had said on several occasions. In fact, after beginning to work with cadavers she insisted on repeating that fact as if she had no connection to the morgue and those bodies.

I was sure the Berabas wouldn't ask for help, perhaps from all the time I'd spent close to Dona Lu. They wanted the body, wanted the burial, wanted to hold a mass and later regularly visit the tomb.

Anyone who hasn't been through it, I told Sulamita more than a hundred times, can't understand. You don't have the faintest idea of what a death without a body is.

Of course I do, it's like a crime without a body: it doesn't exist.

It's more than that, it's like being in purgatory. There are days when you accept that the person is dead. Then you cry and pray. At other times, you hear a sound at the door and think he's come back. You run to the living room and there's no one there. And if the phone rings in the middle of the night you pick it up, full of hope. And you never stop suffering. Or believing. Life doesn't matter anymore, but you also can't die completely, because there's always the possibility of the door opening or the telephone ringing. And you want to be there when it happens.

After seventeen calls making threats, the moment had come for the ransom, and we knew it. We barely slept that night.

The day before, I had called José Beraba demanding that he rent the car with license plate 3422 from the Panorama agency. Sulamita didn't want José Beraba to use one of the family's luxurious and flashy vehicles for the operation, and we had taken care to verify the plate numbers of the available cars at the rental agency.

Sulamita continued delving into what she called "technical questions." Now, when she aired her ideas and theories, she said "I" and "you." I did the same thing, I thought. At the beginning there was a certain reserve on our part, we didn't speak in such personal terms, there wasn't any "I" or "you," just the fisherman. The fisherman who called the Berabas late at night. And made threats. Now, I thought, we were that fisherman.

Before leaving the bakery, Sulamita told me that at the end of the afternoon she'd bring her uncle's car for the operation. It's better for it to stay with you. I'll take a taxi, she said.

I walked with her to the bus stop.

I love you, she said.

In such situations I always felt obliged to say "Me too." And I always remembered Rita. "Me too," Rita used to say. It's the response of someone who feels nothing.

Here comes your bus, I told Sulamita.

Do you love me?

Yes, I answered.

Then say it.

I already did.

Say: "Sulamita, I love you."

Sulamita, I love you.

She got on the bus and waved at me from the window, smiling, making me feel like a rat.

I went home to get the car, and before going to work I stopped by Eliana's.

Talk to your Indian, she said when I gave her money for purchases. That crazy woman refuses to eat, she just sits there with that imbecilic look on her face, and I've got two kids to take care of.

Serafina was sad, in the corner of the kitchen, huddled in a chair, her coarse ugly hands entwined in her lap. I felt enormous affection for her. I kneeled beside her and asked for a little more patience. Just a few more days and I'll take you away from here, I said. You're going to live with me and Sulamita.

She smiled. I think it was the first time I ever saw Serafina smile.

There weren't many teeth in her mouth.

33

The day was a long one. All I could feel was a wordless tension that left my nerves in tatters. I spent the entire time alone in the garage. I wasn't asked to do anything, I did absolutely nothing besides drink coffee with Dalva and chat with the pool man.

At certain moments I was totally convinced I should give up on our plan. I thought about Dona Lu and how she was suffering, and how all of it was similar to the ordeal my mother had gone through. The alternatives were complicated, I thought.

Killing Ramirez and Juan, running away to Rita, arranging false documents. I said to myself, Get out, over. But it was too late. My clandestine radio was off the air. Over and out. There wasn't anyone more inside me. I ruled, I decided. Just me.

At eight that evening Sulamita was on watch at the bus station.

Half an hour earlier, at home, we had reviewed the plan thoroughly, but she went on asking me the same questions.

Are you sure? she asked by phone.

I'm sure, I said.

Only say what's necessary. And disguise your voice. When you make contact, talk as if you were hoarse. Do exactly what we agreed. I'm going to keep tabs on the precinct by phone.

You already told me all that.

Is Junior's cell phone charged?

Fully charged.

I love you, she said.

Me too.

No matter what happens, we're in this together.

That's fine, I said, I gotta go.

At 8.10 p.m. I called José Beraba and told him to go by himself to the bus station and look for the public phones near the ticket window. Get in the rental car, I said. There's an envelope taped under the first telephone. Just follow the instructions.

Sulamita called me at 8.45 p.m. It's clear, she said. José Beraba is by himself. I'm taking a taxi to the gas station.

In the envelope were instructions for José Beraba to drive to the Krispan supermarket and look for a red piece of paper under the trash can to the right of the entrance.

I was waiting in the supermarket parking lot in Sulamita's aunt's car, an old VW whose tinted windows prevented me being seen from the outside.

Underneath the trash can we placed the following directions:

"Take Highway 26A to Kilometer 34. Wait for phone call."

We set up a kind of treasure hunt, and Sulamita told me that was how kidnappers operated. You have to get the victim dazed, she said, and at the same time check how he acts at different stages. If the police are involved, we'll know.

Sulamita, who was already at the gas station at the entrance to 26A, phoned me when she saw Beraba's rental car heading toward Kilometer 34.

Ten minutes later, I arrived at the gas station. Sulamita got in the car, panting. Park back there, she said, pointing to a more protected area.

Then she called Joel at the precinct, with the excuse that she needed the number of a mutual friend. Sweetheart, he said, is there anything you ask me with a smile that I don't do for you? he said. Don't suck up to me, Tranqueira, just give me the information. Before hanging up, she also asked to speak with Dudu.

The whole team's there, having their Friday night beer bust, she said when she hung up.

We waited a few minutes and then I called José Beraba's cell phone again. I told him to walk to the third lamp post on the highway, to his left, where there was an envelope with more instructions, beneath a rectangular stone.

Sulamita, always thinking of forensics, had prepared all the notes that afternoon. The final one read: "Take the side road at Kilometer 42. Park the car. Go four hundred meters toward Green Creek and wait there with the headlights off."

We went toward the side road, taking a shortcut that started at the same abandoned farm where we had buried our cadaver. The shortcut came out at Green Creek on the other side of 26A. We hid the car behind a thicket and waited a bit, looking at the road, which was now just below us. From there we could see any vehicle that approached.

Minutes later we saw a car enter the side road and turn off its headlights. I called José Beraba again.

I'm already there, he said. It's very dark; I can't see anything.

Drive three hundred meters. You'll find a crossroad. Wait inside the car. With the lights off, I ordered.

I put on the mask and said goodbye to Sulamita. Wait until I turn on the headlights, I said before starting my walk.

I had already covered the same course three times with Sulamita, but at night things were very different. I walked carefully, afraid I would hurt myself. The darkness, however, was our guarantee. If any car approached, we would abort the operation. It took me over ten minutes to get to the crossroad.

José Beraba was inside the car. Only then did I turn on the flashlight, signaling. I kept the beam of light on the rancher's face, blinding him. As soon as he got out of the car I asked where the money was.

In the valise on the front seat, the passenger side, he said.

I turned off the flashlight, went to the car, opened and closed the door twice as if there were more people with me.

Don't call the police, I said. Keep your cell phone on.

What about my son? he asked.

You'll receive instructions.

I added that he was to go on until he got to the main road. It's an hour's walk, I said.

I turned on the headlights and took off at high speed.

It was like having no arms or legs. Tires, steering wheel, head, ideas, nothing. Just my heart beating out of control. I recalled the CD I had received from Rita two days ago. Like always, no return address. On it, an ultrasound image with the same black dot, but this time with sound. *Toom toom toom*, the creature pulsated. I spent half an hour at an Internet café downtown, listening to those heartbeats. Now, driving in the darkness, I felt like that black dot. A heart in the dark, nothing more. Pulsating.

At the agreed-upon location, Sulamita was waiting for me in the VW. I parked beside her, under a tree. No sign of movement, no one. Everything's fine, she said, coming over to my window. I opened the valise, wearing gloves, and transferred the money to a garbage bag she had brought. Then I left the valise in the rental car and put the key on top of one of the tires the way parking valets do.

Sulamita ran a cloth over the panel and locks to wipe away my fingerprints.

On the way home, using Junior's cell phone, I called José Beraba again and explained where he could find the rental car and where I'd left the ignition key.

If you keep on cooperating you'll have your son back soon, I said.

We arrived home at 10.20 p.m.

Sulamita spread the money on top of the bed and started saying holy shit. Holy shit, she repeated as she walked around the bed.

Holy shit. I couldn't believe it myself.

34

Good morning, man of the Pantanal, said Sulamita when we woke on Saturday. Now that we're almost rich, she said, all I want is some peace.

After returning the car to Sulamita's aunt, we went to the outdoor market in shorts and sandals with a list of purchases her mother had given by phone.

My father-in-law had stocked the refrigerator with beer and we spent Saturday around the barbecue grill.

I've never seen you drink so much, the old man told Sulamita.

Regina was happy on such occasions, shouting and thrashing around like some caged animal. At times her screams disturbed me. Calm your sister down, I asked Sulamita.

Around ten that night, when we were mellowed out on the living room sofa, watching television, Sulamita, hanging onto my neck, said she wanted to dance.

Where? I asked.

I don't know, wherever.

I've always hated nightclubs, I explained.

You don't understand. I need to. It's a real necessity.

I waited for Sulamita to bathe and get dolled up, and we went to a discotheque in the city, a veritable oven, with techno music that shattered my eardrums. She continued to hit the booze and at one point disappeared into the crowd entirely. I didn't find her till half an hour later, dancing by herself, eyes closed, no rhythm, ignoring the music. When I approached, I saw she was crying. Enough, Sulamita, we've celebrated enough, I said.

I woke up Sunday with a dull pain in the back of my neck and a dry sandpaper tongue as if I'd eaten dirt. My eyes burned and I could barely sit up in bed. Sulamita, already showered, brought me a cup of coffee that Serafina had made. She was about to leave for her shift at the morgue.

Call now, she said. I want to leave with everything taken care of.

At noon precisely I called José Beraba and gave detailed information about where Junior's body was buried. There's a white fence post, I said, half a meter high, marking the spot.

He was silent.

Did you hear me? I asked.

Yes, he said. I can't believe it. You want me to dig up my own son, you piece of shit?

I hung up, not understanding.

What did he want us to do? asked Sulamita. Deliver the body to his house? Send it by mail?

She sighed, distressed.

Get rid of Junior's phone, she said. Throw it in the river. I'm leaving. I need to be there when everything happens.

And this is how everything happened:

José Beraba went with Dona Lu to the place we indicated. From there, even before opening the grave, he called Pedro Caleiro and asked the precinct chief to meet him.

Caleiro, after being apprised of the matter, called Joel and Dudu, along with the hostage team.

By five o'clock the body was at the morgue. I received it myself, Sulamita told me when she returned from work at eleven that night.

We were now in my bed, facing each other, holding hands.

How much do they know? I asked.

I know Joel well and know he's suspicious. I sounded out Caleiro and Dudu. Both told me the family still hasn't made it totally clear how the body was found. What does that mean?

If it's up to Dona Lu, they won't want to follow protocol.

That's where you're wrong, said Sulamita. The collection of genetic material from the family to identify the body is already scheduled for tomorrow. I have to find a way to be the one who takes the material to the lab in Brasilia.

And what if you can't?

I'll go anyway, even if it has to be secretly and at my own expense. My impression, she said, is that José Beraba is hiding something. But I could be wrong. Maybe Caleiro knows everything and wants to keep the investigation confidential; that also happens. In fact, Caleiro remained at the morgue the whole time, which isn't usual.

What are we going to do? I asked.

Until the material is collected, nothing.

And then?

Everything goes on like before. Our fate is in the hands of my friend.

She was referring to the worker who wrote up the reports from the laboratory in Brasilia, the one we would try to bribe.

What if he doesn't go for it? What if he turns us in? I bombarded Sulamita with questions, but unlike me she didn't seem worried about the tests. What she was concerned about was Joel's behavior. He's been talking strangely, she said. Asking questions about you and your job. He also said he's having some financial difficulties. Odd, don't you think?

172

35

The next day, Sulamita called as soon as she got to work, around seven. It's obvious, she said, that there's been a lot of movement here during the night. I saw X-rays from Junior's dentist on Rosana's desk, which isn't going to prove anything because I smashed the dental arches before we buried the body. But how did they get access to those X-rays late Sunday night? The Berabas are cooperating, just the opposite of what we imagined. They phoned the dentist. The question is: which version have they told the police? What does Pedro Caleiro know?

There was another complication, according to Sulamita. Rosana, the coroner in charge, hadn't passed along any information. We always talk about the cases, she said, and this time I sensed a certain holding back.

We hung up after I promised to feel out the terrain and, above all, not to do anything stupid. I need to be sure, she said, that you're in control.

I had a hard time getting up; the night had been infernal. We had stayed up talking till late, replete in extreme agony with hypotheses we had never considered. What if we'd left footprints at the site where we buried the cadaver? What if our phones were tapped? What if someone had seen us? And what if the police knew everything all along?

There was a moment when I was so desperate that I tried to convince Sulamita that we should turn ourselves in. We would return the ransom money and I would rat out Ramirez. That would weigh in our favor at our trial. You said yourself there's no such thing as a perfect crime. They're going to find out.

What I know is that there are bungled investigations, she replied. I'm on the inside and see a lot of sloppy practices. I know how things work. There are many ways to sabotage an investigation.

By morning, Sulamita had managed to calm me down by saying there'd be no problem at all if we were suspected. Nobody goes to jail for being suspected of a crime, she said. What they can't be allowed to do is establish proof.

I felt exhausted, without the strength to resist what was ahead, but even so, I followed her instructions to the letter.

I arrived at the Berabas' early. The pool was covered with leaves, and clearing them away was an activity that served to calm me. From poolside, holding a strainer with a long handle, I cleaned carefully.

Dalva brought me coffee. They found Junior, she said, confused. Did Sulamita tell you anything?

Nothing, I said, emptying the strainer in the garden.

What does she think of the whole thing?

She was on duty yesterday, I answered. We haven't had a chance to talk.

Dalva looked at me as if she didn't believe me.

You didn't ask anything?

I set the strainer down and sighed.

The police must have a machine, Dalva said, I don't know, some way to tell if it's really Junior. I've seen it on TV.

I was rescued by Dona Lu, who signaled from the window of Junior's room for me to come there.

I went into the house, agitated, my thoughts going from that pulsating black spot in Rita's belly to Sulamita's agile hands breaking the cadaver's bones, while I repeated to myself that they knew nothing, over, I hadn't killed anyone, there was no way they'd catch me.

In the bedroom Dona Lu, looking better than usual, asked if I'd heard the news, and before I could reply she threw open the door of the built-in wardrobe and said she had decided to donate her son's clothes to charity. Choose anything you'd like, she said before leaving me by myself. You're about the same size.

As I separated a few items, pants, shirts, I remembered that until the day she died, twenty years after my father's disappearance, my mother kept her husband's closet intact. It's true, I thought, trying on a red T-shirt, Junior's death is happening at this very moment, and I felt happy for Dona Lu. You could see a certain relief in her expression. She's finally free, I thought.

And it was then, out the window, that I saw the precinct chief Pedro Caleiro coming through the garden, accompanied by Joel and Dudu.

I ran to the bathroom, turned on the faucet and threw cold water on my face, trying to calm myself. It's not the only test we plan to run, I heard someone say minutes later. Junior's bathroom was next to José Beraba's office, with both looking out onto the front garden of the house. I closed the bedroom door and carefully opened the bathroom window, but even then it wasn't possible to hear clearly what they were saying.

I went back to the bedroom and called Sulamita.

Try to listen to what they're saying, she said. I've found out it was José Beraba who called the meeting there. I imagine they're going to talk about the tests. Try to find out.

I hung up the cell phone, chose some clothes at random from the wardrobe, left them in the small outbuilding, and went to chat with the pool man, offering to help him in the garden.

With the garden shears, I approached the window of José Beraba's office without getting so close as to appear indiscreet. What I heard was stray bits of sentences: My wife is living on tranquilizers. Expand the investigation. Inconvenient. Employees. Another way of resolving. Employees. Interrogations. Dalva. Interests. Employees.

What made me uneasy was hearing the word employees several times, always uttered by Caleiro.

And it was like that, squatting, pretending to trim the grass, that I saw Joel's boots approaching. You take care of the garden too? he asked.

I rose quickly and felt my vision go dark.

Helping out, I answered.

It's very good to have friends who help, he said.

I didn't like Joel's manner. A bit arrogant, standing with his hands on his waist, without looking at me directly.

It's my job, I said.

Who's talking about work? he asked, a malign smile on his lips. I'm talking about friends. Real friends. People who cover for you. I myself have lots of friends. Sulamita, for example. She's my friend. I mean, I think we're friends.

And he laughed.

What did you two do on the weekend?

We went dancing, I said.

He looked at me suspiciously.

What a macabre story, eh?

Very, I said.

We're going to have to call you in to make a statement, he said.

I remained silent.

Dalva appeared in the garden and asked me to get Dona Lu's car ready. I said goodbye to Joel and headed for the garage, my heart almost leaping out of my mouth.

The Martins & Sons Funeral Home.

Urns, wreaths, candleholders, prayer beads – the products were displayed like kitchen appliances. Not even death escapes the tactics of business. There are people who lie in the coffin to try it out. There are people who buy with an eye to the future. That's what Martins' son told me as I waited on the sidewalk for Dona Lu. I wanted to be by myself, to call Sulamita, find out what the hell was happening, but the young man wouldn't stop talking, and when he finally figured out I wasn't in the mood for idle chitchat, Dona Lu signaled for me to come help her.

Do you like it? she asked, showing me a dark, overly ornamented casket.

I prefer this one, I replied.

It's more discreet, she said. You're right.

Afterward, we went to the church, where she had a meeting with Father Alfredo to talk about the wake and the mass. Come in with me, she said as I parked. I need your help.

Despite her behavior not indicating she suspected me, I couldn't calm down. What had Joel been insinuating with that talk about friends? What did he know?

Back at the Berabas', as soon as Dona Lu got out of the car I phoned Sulamita at the morgue.

There's no one here, said the operator. They were all called to an emergency meeting at the precinct.

36

You know what I'm going to do with this piece of crap? Do you?

I was at the window, out of control, a knife in one hand and the soccer ball in the other. The boys in the street looked at me, scared. Overcome with fury, I stabbed the ball in several places and tossed the wilted leather hull back onto the asphalt.

Jeez, said one of the Indian kids, it was a professional soccer ball. Alceu bought it for us.

It was after eight at night, and the kids had just broken my window. Generally, I was patient with the little Guatós, but that night my nerves were rubbed raw. After my outburst, the noise stopped, but I could still hear some mews of unhappiness as I attempted to find out what had happened with Sulamita. I had phoned the morgue more than twenty times, and she still hadn't returned from that meeting. What the fuck kind of meeting was it? What was going on? Why had she turned off her cell?

I paced the room, in circles, with the feeling that something bad was about to happen. The kids called me to talk at the window. Jeez, they said. They said, Forgive us. Jeez, they said, darn. I ended up giving them the money to buy another ball. But play a long way from here, I said.

Shortly afterward, Sulamita called. Come to the precinct, she said. There's no describing the fear I felt en route. It was more like a breakdown, a collapse; I sweated, trembled, my heart raced. I thought, maybe I'm having a coronary. On the radio, the reporter said: São Paulo is still flooded. I imagined the poor in water up to their waists. Furniture floating in the streets. Refrigerators, television sets. The reporter said: Three Muslims flogged in Malaysia for adultery. I imagined the welts on their skin. The reporter said: Court upholds impeachment of the governor. So far, so good, I thought. I'm not in São Paulo. I'm not a Muslim. Or the governor.

When I parked, Joel was standing at the door of the station.

Come to give yourself up? he asked.

It occurred to me at that moment that Sulamita had betrayed me. And then Joel guffawed. You lucky guy, he said.

I don't know how long I stayed in the van, but Joel, smoking on the sidewalk, never took his eyes off me for a second. When Sulamita got in the car, I took off abruptly, and as soon as I turned the corner started shouting Fuck, how could you do that to me? Where'd you disappear to? What the fuck is happening? I roared, slamming my fist against the dashboard.

They've closed the case, she said, taking from her purse a wad of bills she had just gotten from the chief.

Livid, I parked the car in Central Square to hear the rest of the story. I found out early this afternoon that the investigation had been called off, said Sulamita. I had already phoned my friend in Brasilia. Good thing I didn't bring up the subject.

Sulamita added that it had been Dudu who called her to the meeting at the station. Caleiro was there, she said, they asked questions about you, about the two of us, blah blah blah. They talked and talked without saying anything. Then I asked when we would have the material from the family for the tests in Brasilia. The two of them got even more flustered. They said we needed to respect the family's suffering and blah blah blah, and I finally understood why they'd called me there. Beraba himself doesn't want the test done to identify the body. To spare his wife.

They're not going to do the test?

The rich have their own laws. Case closed. And I, as a member of the team, have to keep my mouth shut. What they wanted to know was my price. We opened a negotiation. Telling it like that, it may seem like we were businessmen talking about sales. But the thing is quite sophisticated. Those guys know how to bribe. They're very efficient and do it in such a way that you're unaware you're being corrupted. Actually, you even believe you're doing them a favor. Helping. The word money was never mentioned. We talked about compensation and collaboration. Facilitation. And mutual benefit. That's how things are done in this country.

What about Joel? I asked.

As soon as I got to the station he took me aside and asked who my partners were. Just like that, out of nowhere. With the expression of someone who's joking but speaking seriously, you know? I told him my partner was the owner of a junkyard and a cocaine trafficker. You should've seen his face. He wilted immediately. He understood my message perfectly.

Is that it? I asked.

C'est fini, she replied.

We remained silent for a moment, holding hands. Give me a kiss, she said, and take me home.

First, I opened the window. I needed air.

37

The suitcase was opened and the dollars were there. Sixty thousand.

Juan started to count them, greedily. The scene was disgusting. He took apart the bundles of money, methodically piling the bills, all the time wetting his fingers with saliva, as if feasting on delicacies.

Ramirez looked at me with satisfaction. His hair, flattened and rebellious, now seemed like an old, useless brush.

Sit down. Want something to drink, Porco?

I thanked him.

Funny thing, he said, I forgot your name.

You can go on calling me Porco, I said.

Porco, of course. Now that we trust each other, Porco, we can grow our business.

We smiled.

We were in the kitchen of his laboratory in Puerto Suárez. Ramirez said that Corumbá was only the route for cocaine coming from Bolivia and that all the Colombian drugs entered Brazil through Paraguay. We can grow your business, he repeated, adding that now they had a partner in Paraguay and needed someone like me to get the drug into Brazil. I don't need mules, he said. I need brains. It's a great deal for you; extradition from Paraguay is real complicated. I can guarantee there ain't no risks.

I wasn't the least bit interested in what Ramirez was saying, and he went on talking and I went on reading the newspaper I'd brought with me, where there was an item saying that Junior's body had been found. The official version was that a farmer had noticed a strange smell on his land and had discovered the cadaver in a thicket. The police "believed" that Junior had left the airplane, wounded, and had died trying to find help.

I continued reading the paper, and Ramirez wouldn't shut up. Out of every ten words, one was Porco. Porco chum. Porco friend. I ran my eyes over the other headlines. "Covered in a burka, Afghan woman displays her dirty finger after voting." Goddamn, I thought, I've never seen so many ugly words together. Burka. Dirty finger.

It's all there, said Juan, who had finished counting the money.

Before I left, Ramirez put his hand on my shoulder and asked me to think about his offer. He also said it hadn't been him who killed Moacir. I found out he really did kill himself, he said.

It's sad, he said. The truth is, Porco, that good people always end up dying.

Now, I thought on my way back to Corumbá, I don't have anybody on my neck. Free, over.

38

The wake was a grand event.

The coffin was closed, and there were so many flowers that from outside the church you could already smell a sweetish aroma in the air.

The entire city showed up. Most of those present had no direct connection to the family, curious types who followed the news on television and were there for their own amusement. There were eulogies and weeping.

Dona Lu received the condolences and I could see, behind her mourning attire and her controlled expression, a certain peace.

Sulamita and I also went to the funeral the next morning.

The day was sunny.

I noticed that the gravedigger who'd done Junior's sepulcher was the same one who had sold us the cadaver,

At the end of the ceremony, we gave our condolences to Dona Lu and Mr. José.

Thank you very much, they said.

We left through the passageways of the cemetery, hand in hand, feeling the sun hot upon our dark clothing.

39

The next morning, when I arrived at work, Dona Lu was in a T-shirt and overalls, puttering in the garden. I'm going to plant azaleas, she said.

In the kitchen, Dalva didn't offer me coffee as she normally did. And when I asked her for a cup, she pointed to the thermos bottle. Get it yourself, she said, I'm busy.

Is there some problem? I asked.

She smiled in an odd way, a bit cynically, and said that José Beraba was waiting for me in the office.

I found him working, behind his desk. He didn't greet me or even raise his eyes to speak to me.

It's all here, he said, your severance pay, all that's missing is your signature on the paperwork. Starting today, you're no longer in my employ.

I started to say something, but he interrupted me. Listen carefully to what I'm about to say. You're going to leave here right now, you're going to call Dona Lu and say you've resigned. Tell her that beginning today you can't work anymore. Tell her you're getting married, you've got cancer, or make up some lie.

I stood there looking at the severance check, paralyzed.

Sign here, he said.

While I signed the receipts in a shaky hand, José Beraba went on talking. I couldn't bring myself to look at him.

If it weren't for my wife, he said, my sainted wife, if it

weren't for her health, I swear to you everything would have been different. I would have put a bullet in your cynical face myself.

I handed him the papers.

Get out of my house, you worm. That's what you are. A worm.

And he didn't even wait for me to go. He left me standing there, hearing the sound of his boots echoing on the floor.

Epilogue

One year later

The cow didn't look well, and I was concerned. She was a present from Dona Lu for our wedding, a purebred, and I didn't want to take any chances.

Get a rope, I told my father-in-law.

Regina, who had come to the stable with Serafina to witness the birth, yelled in distress. Take her out of here, I said to Serafina, we're not going to upset the cow even more.

My father-in-law brought the rope and we tied the calf's legs, which were partially outside its mother's belly. I carefully pulled them, and gradually the calf emerged, along with the placenta.

It's a female, I said.

In the afternoon, after lunch, I went to the city with a list of purchases that Sulamita had given me.

In the supermarket I ran into Eliana.

It's been a long time, I said. Eliana was pregnant and married to Alceu.

I asked about the children.

Good, she said. I've got an envelope for you at home. It came some time ago; I didn't know how to find you.

I gave her and Alceu a lift, and when we got to her house she gave me the envelope.

I opened it and saw a photo of Rita, in a bikini, with a little girl in her lap and the two of them having ice cream at the beach.

"If you want to meet your daughter, we're here. Life in Rio is wonderful, it has nothing to do with the smell of cow dung, or that collection of rednecks in Corumbá."

I stood there on the sidewalk, looking at the photo. Damn, Rita, the girl looks like me. I burned the photo, with a heavy heart. Who can predict the turns the world takes?

When I arrived at the ranch, Sulamita was in the garden, with Regina and her mother. Her belly was large; our child would be born in two months.

Did you see the palms I planted? Sulamita asked, showing me the seedlings. A green meadow stretched into the distance, with small copses the previous owner had planted.

The sun was setting and a pleasant breeze was blowing in our direction.

I sat down beside them to savor the landscape. There's no place prettier than the Pantanal, I said.

Those palms are really lovely, said my mother-in-law, offering me a cold lemonade.

Frjshsg, Regina grunted.

Did you hear? She said "palm," Sulamita said. That's right, darling. Palms, she repeated. The palms *are* beautiful.

Acknowledgments

I thank Jane Pacheco Bellucci and Roberta Astolfi for invaluable collaboration in the research. I also thank my editor, Paulo Rocco, and Marianna Teixeira Soares for their support and enthusiasm. As always, special thanks to my eternal friend Rubem Fonseca for his attentive reading, and to my husband John for being ever at my side.

The Body Snatcher is a work of fiction, with names of characters and places freely created by the author, with no relation to reality.